MIND'S EYE

THE SKYWARD SAGA

BOOK 2

A.R. KNIGHT

1 / NEW EMPIRES

The black pool burbles, pops and roils in front of me. A pair of tanned, cloth-wrapped workers sweep long-handled poles through the same mix that had brought my god to me, keeping what's inside churning, bringing it closer to what we need.

Well done.

I'm smiling as I look around the chamber, walls lined with lit torches, and see a second pool slowly filling as more workers dump buckets of the mixture into a stone pit. Alchemists create each new batch of the mix; a blend of plants, minerals, and water.

My fellow gods will be happy. Proud of what you've made.

Ignos talks about his fellow gods a lot now, but that's not the only thing that's changed.

With the Cache, the people who call me Empress are crafting one miracle after the next. It's like watching a fire-burned jungle grow: something wholly different emerges from the landscape. My people, our world is changing. The words taste strange to me. *My people.* The Charre were, not long ago, enemies. Or, at best, adversaries to be wary of when they crashed through the jungle to my village.

Now, they scream my name when I walk the markets. They drink every word I preach. Take my every order as a dream.

Months ago, I was a sixteen year-old girl with no real future. A small tribe Solare waiting for something to happen. Now, I'm getting called by a pair of priests and told it's time to lead a ceremony.

I leave the pools, following the trail of torches up and out of the temple. When Ignos tells me they're ready, we'll use a device my metalworkers are making to send a message to where the other gods are staying. We'll tell them that it's time to come home.

When the rest of the gods arrive, then truly everyone will see as I have seen, will know what I know, and all of my people will be saved.

I don't know about that part, but not having to struggle for food, not having to carve out the hearts of captives and pray for rain, that sounds pretty good.

Still, I'm not an Empress of nothing. Evidence of my people's prowess is on display as I climb the hard stone steps into the Vaos' main chamber. The windows on either side let light in from precise angles so that a golden glow fills everything. Heat comes with it, comforting after the cool air underground. Incense, burning in several small vials around the chamber, hides the musk of a city in full growth.

There's something new hanging on the walls: three clear globes with black bases latched to the stone. I go to the first one and press a small round, raised area close to its bottom. The globe flickers, green sparks popping up from inside it. After a moment, they steady, keeping up a cascade that brightens the room.

"A sparker, Empress," says one of the ever-present priests awaiting my command. "A new miracle, though this one of our own making."

"Our own?"

"The inventor took what the Cache provided and made her own modifications, Empress." The priest bows deep. "She mentioned that if you wish it to stop, all you need is to release the button."

I do so, and the sparks die off immediately. "Tell this inventor to come here soon. I need to congratulate her."

Your people are growing up, Empress. I am impressed.

I smile at the voice in my head. Ignos doesn't talk as much these days. He is, he tells me, pulling and weeding through more of the information from the Cache. Once the pools are ready, things will move quickly and he needs to be prepared. When I ask him for what, he doesn't reply.

I like it when he talks to me. Ignos is the only one who truly knows, after all, who I am. Where I came from. He keeps our grand show going. Keeps my people from finding out who I really am.

I reach up and adjust the emerald headdress so that it fits more comfortably. The shawl on my shoulders is similarly green, an homage to where I came from. One of the few I allow myself. I can't be seen as a Solare. I can't be seen as less than the people I lead.

"They are ready for you." My lead general and commander, and my friend, Malo joins me in the chamber. To the lion's mane framing his face and shoulders, he's added a fine white and gold robe, a symbol of his rank. I think he looks better in the plain skirt of a fighter, but then, I come from a simple village. "Only adoration today, Empress."

"Don't call me that," I reply. "You know my name."

Malo quirks a smile. "I do. But now, especially right now, you have to be a leader. And a leader needs her title."

I don't argue, because he's right, as he is about most things. So I follow Malo as he walks ahead of me. As soon as he appears at the threshold to the great steps, their mottled gray stone sprawling in front of him, horns blow. A cheer rises up, one that continues and grows as I join Malo. As I raise my hands to the crowd.

Thousands throng into the square around the Vaos. For a moment I can't resist, and look up behind me at the twin altars, up those many steps. They glow in the noonday light of Ignos. Each of those altars holds a prisoner. Ones caught plotting against me.

Not every Charre likes the thought of me leading their empire.

Once, I'd wanted to end the sacrifices. I'd never relished holding the black glass knife, making the cuts. Ignos, though, warned me to wait. Told me that such ceremonies might be useful. He is right.

I walk up the steps, the crowd cheering behind me. Today, I'm grateful. I won't be wielding the knife. Instead, a pair of younger priests carry the burden. New ones in my order, and they'll be doing the slicing.

I watch, and occasionally look over the sea of smiling, cheering faces, and this time when I speak the rites and prayers, I add new ones. I tell my followers to believe, to get ready, because their time is nearly here.

Ignos is coming for them.

2 / THE HUNTERS

Sax admits that this is one of the prettier planets he's ever seen. From space, the swirling whites layer over large swaths of blue give contrast with the brown and green continents. The colors of life.

And life mixed with the Sevora means danger.

"Briefing, how long have the Sevora been here?" Bas, his pair, asks the line of terminals in front of her rose-gold body. Much more fascinating than Sax's own gleaming gray, one of many reasons why Sax is infinitely happy Bas shares his existence.

They're standing in the bridge of their craft. A shuttle they've been squeezed into, seeing as Oratus are massive creatures. Four clawed arms, two taloned legs, and a tail, all covered in hard scales, makes for awkward seating arrangements.

Bas is talking to the shuttle, to a briefing program and the windshield's sudden shimmer starts its response. The program scans its available data for an answer, then flashes green as it finds one and molds it into a conversational phrase.

"Less than a single local orbit," the program replies in the voice of Evva, their commander. "By conventional measures, and the estimated technological level of this planet, you have enough time to interrupt the process."

Sevora move quickly to establish their foothold, to capture a race and build their infrastructure. If the planet is truly primitive, it can take longer. Sax, though, is more surprised at the look of this planet than anything. Atmospheric scans and visual data indicate a world rich in resources, with a hospitable climate.

It's surprising the world isn't already settled, inducted into the galaxy at large.

"Evva, why is this an unknown planet? We're not on the fringes." Sax addresses the program as if he's talking to his commander.

It's easier that way.

The windshield flashes red a second later. No logged answers.

"Transmit question," Sax says and the program beeps acknowledgment.

Evva's ship is a long way from here. Light-years. The briefing programs use quantum tuning to leap the distances—micro changes in this shuttle's program shift the designated one on Evva's ship—but the process takes time. Every letter of Sax's question would be sent one by one, registered by Evva's program, and then Evva's answer, when she chose to send it, would be received by the shuttle in the same way.

It's why memory dumps are more efficient—simply spew everything about a given mission into the designated briefing program before leaping away and make it easier for the team to look things up.

Of course, this is only necessary because the Vincere forces split up. They destroyed the last seed ship—a mobile Sevora breeding ground—and now Sax and Bas have to clean up a Sevora that escaped.

Which is why the Oratus have come; One Sevora, left alone, can rebuild the entire race. It's happened before.

From orbit, they spend revolutions scanning the planet and find the only real concentration of civilization is in a broad belt just north of its equator. An East-West stretch that covers a range of climates.

They pick up structures, movement, and even some signs of energy use. It's strange to see life so concentrated in this one part when there's a whole world to explore, but Sax isn't here to ask questions. Isn't here to learn why these people chose to do as they have. He's here to make sure they can continue to make their own choices.

And if they can't, he'll save them from that fate too.

3 / IGNOS' BOUNTY

The high, healthy stalks signal a great harvest is on the way. I point across a rolling hill, covered in yellow wheat, towards a roving herd of goats farther off in the distance. There are several dozen of them, roaming around a couple of shepherds. If I had a pair of the new telescopic eyeglasses our metalworkers are making, I could likely see the silver collars around the animals' throats, and the shock-buzzers in the shepherds' hands.

"Are they yours too?" I ask the man standing next to me, who laughs.

There's real joy in that laughter, a big-hearted chuckle that says more about the state of my people than anything else.

"No, Empress. I tend the crops, and they tend to the goats. In exchange, I give them food and they give me milk. It works for the both of us."

"It works for the Charre," Viera, standing behind me in her emerald leather armor, hand perennially on her pistol hilt, says. "Looks like you're having quite the year."

The farmer laughs again, dishes Viera a knowing look to say he doesn't begrudge his own success. "It's been a wonderful year for everyone. Ignos has favored us, and the alchemists' fertilizer has made our stalks grow tall, hard, and strong. This season will be the best we've ever had. Not one in Damantum will starve."

"And none of your purses will be empty," I say. The farmer nods, but says nothing else.

Societies must either be desperate or thriving before they'll invest in something new. Be happy yours is on the latter side of that equation.

"Have we seen enough for one day?" Viera asks.

We've been visiting the major landholdings outside of the city. Crawling up and down the wide sloping hills and mountains that overlook the glorious metropolis that I now name my home. Damantum, city of thousands upon thousands, all of whom call me, whether they wish to or not, Empress.

I'm still not used to surroundings of brick and stone, and the chance to get out of the city, feel the wind in the wild free air instead of the stultifying smells of sulfur and waste, has been a treasure. One I'd rather not relinquish until I have to.

"Are there anymore?" I say, both to Viera and the farmer.

"Depends, Empress," the farmer says. "There's not many who wouldn't step outside to thank you. But most of us, especially as Ignos draws down, have to see about feeding our own families. Finishing our chores. Life out here doesn't wait for ceremony."

"You'll wait on your Empress just the same," Viera says.

"Of course, of course, I didn't mean to imply any disrespect," the farmer looks at his hands. Wrinkled and calloused, though he himself is not that old. "What I only mean to say, is my wife, my children, they will be missing me."

I shade my eyes, look to where Ignos is bleeding down towards the horizon. The act reminds me of the four guards standing near us. My Shadows, Malo calls them. A permanent part of my life, especially after Jakkan, the former high priest, hired assassins to kill me. Ferociously loyal, Malo says. Personally reviewed by himself. I trust them.

I trust Viera too; a Lunare traitor who, nonetheless, has helped me become who I am. As I look at her, what really holds my attention, what draws a frown to my face, is the pistol looped through a leather belt on her waist.

We are advancing through ages. Faster than you could ever imagine. Guns are a necessary evil. Simple, deadly. They'll keep you alive long enough to get to better ways of waging war.

Though, with the Lunare driven back, I don't know who we're going to be fighting against. It's clear my people don't either–there's been parties in the streets. Celebrations. Trade is booming with the jungle tribes and new routes are opening to peoples in the West and North. It's a good time to be a Charre. It's a good time to be an Empress.

4 / FIRST ENCOUNTER

They land the shuttle in the dark of night over the crater where the seed crashed. Bas found the site from orbit—a rippling, fresh pit where the devastation from the strike is still visible beneath new growth.

It's clear to Sax, as soon as the boarding ramp goes down, that the seed hit some time ago. It's already overgrown with small plants and ferns. Vines stretch around the mottled gray outside of the craft. A small nest of furry creature scatters as Sax claws his way to the ship.

Insects cluster around him, drawn by the shuttle's low blue lights, which provide visibility without being overly conspicuous. Sax brushes away the foliage. Confirms that the seed opened. Confirms that it's empty of the life-sustaining nutrients.

"It's been triggered," Sax says. "The Sevora is gone."

Bas, waiting at the top of the pit, doesn't seem surprised. "We detected plenty of evidence of life on the way here. Likely, someone stumbled upon it."

"It's been here a while, if the growth is consistent with other worlds," Sax replies. "Enough time for the Sevora to immerse itself."

The subtext: the two Oratus have to be ready for resistance.

They return to the shuttle, gear up with a pair of miners—heat-blasting rifles—apiece, and Sax grabs his black bars, the ones that, if needed, can cut through anything this planet would care to throw at them.

The Oratus head into the jungle. There's no trail, and the thick, snarled plants mean it's been some time since any thing has made its way to the crash site. So, instead, Sax listens. The sounds of the jungle crash over him in waves. The hoots of mysterious creatures, sharp, chirping calls of others, the whistling of wind shooting between tree trunks, making branches and leaves clatter their way from canopy to ground. It's a lovely chorus, even if it doesn't help Sax determine where to go.

But there's something else beneath the sounds—a low, consistent pulse that shakes his legs.

Music.

Bas hears it too, and they both glance at each other, their eyes acknowledging their shared intuition, then head towards the sound. It's slow going—the growth is thick, and the two Oratus commit to staying quiet. It's unclear what kind of resistance they might face, what level of technology. Best to surprise a potential enemy than the other way around.

As they close, the music grows louder, and now there's singing to go with it. Words Sax is surprised to find he recognizes. A cheerful song, of harvests and thanks. Of gifts.

"Sevora gifts," Bas hisses.

Sax agrees. They keep moving and Sax falls into the mystery of the hunt. The strange sweet zone where time dilates and all of his instincts come into focus. Where the slightest whisper of wings feels like the loudest thunderclap.

Which is when he notices they are being tracked.

Sax looks to his left and sees a strange species standing there. Counts two arms, two legs and what appears to be a head growing out of a sizable torso. Smaller than Sax himself. Though, going by the steady eyes staring back at him, this species is not afraid of the Oratus.

The creature holds a short spear, and it angles the weapon towards Sax. Shoves the spear, point first, towards the Oratus. Not close enough to hurt, and Sax recognizes the warning. Step closer, the creature is saying, and that point will make its way into Sax's chest.

Sax's mask would likely turn the spear, and Sax would, doubtless, be able to tear the creature apart. But if Sax can see one, there might be others. Starting an uncertain fight in the dark, risking their lives and health, would be a poor plan.

Though he wouldn't mind if the creature did it first.

"What are you?" the creature says. Sax is momentarily stunned to hear the galactic common tongue spoken on this strange world.

It signals Sevora, and Sax tenses.

"Stop," Bas says as she senses Sax's plan. "No Sevora would ask what we were. It would know, it would react."

She's right. Sax straightens, and notices the creature has fallen into its own battle stance. One hand up to its lips, forming a circular gesture, and the other holding the spear, point toward Sax, low and ready to stab.

"We are visitors," Bas hisses. "Newcomers to your land. Who are you?"

"We? We are the Solare. This is our jungle. Our village. Why have you come?"

Neither Sax nor the warrior relax. Both ready to jump at each other's throats. Bas, though, lets her tail touch Sax's his own. Calm down, the gesture says, don't make enemies we don't need.

"We are called Oratus," Bas answers. "We come from far away. Beyond the sky. We are searching for another who came from the stars. Who promises wonders."

Bas' answer works. The creature steps forward, but as it does so, it raises the short spear's point up. "I'm sorry, but you are too late. Who you were looking for left long ago."

Sax straightens up as well. "The one we're looking for?"

The creature seems to remember something. Its face flicks

towards the village. Towards the music and sound. "I'll take you. There are others here who would be better at explaining than I."

"We would be grateful," Bas says.

They follow the creature through the last bit of jungle. Along the way, they ask and the creature tells them what they are: humans. Their tribe and people named Solare. Men and women, daughters and sons. The man speaks so freely and Sax doesn't understand why until their escort calls them gods.

Ah.

Sax does nothing to dispel the thought.

They head into a wide clearing from which rise a number of crude stone buildings and one strange, tall mass of wood, moss and rock. In front of it appears the rest of the tribe. The whole group of them dancing and chanting around pleasing pits of fire. Roasting meats, fruits and burning incense fill the six breathing vents stitching Sax's chest with smells.

At least for a moment, because all of it stops as soon as Sax and Bas come into the firelight. As soon as everyone stares at them. In the quiet, there in a clearing, Sax picks up rustling from around them. He looks, and at the borders of the village stand other humans, holding bows with arrows aimed at the two Oratus.

They've walked into a trap.

5 / THE WARNING

I put too many peppers on the fish again. The white meat is littered with the green circles, but I can't take them off. Not with Viera watching, her face already breaking out into a grin. So I take the whole thing, the fish, the maize, the peppers and the bits of cabbage and shove it into my mouth. With none of the dignity and refined class that an Empress ought to have. But we're alone, our only company a pair of flickering braziers.

It's the same chamber I used to share with Jakkan. In the Vaos, the grand temple in the middle of Damantum. I haven't made the move to the Emperor's palace yet, and I don't know if I ever will. There's nothing about that place that I like, and all it brings with it are bad memories. Ghosts. Not that I knew the Emperor well, but there's something about going into a dead man's house that feels strange.

Uncomfortable.

The heat builds in my mouth. I meet Viera's mocking stare and suffer through it. The tingling burn coats my cheeks and goes down my throat as I swallow.

Why do you do this to yourself?

I ignore Ignos. This is a moment for concentration. Some battles are won with weapons, some by smarts and sneakiness, but this, this will be won by fortitude.

"You want some of the goat milk?" Viera taunts.

I shake my head. The fire increases to an inferno writhing around my tongue. I don't say a word.

"You sure? I think I see a tear in your eye."

She's not wrong. I feel the moisture on the edges. I blink once. Keep my stare, my smile locked. Finally, finally the spice begins to die. I'm fairly certain I've scalded something, but I'm still alive. Haven't thrown up, haven't spat everywhere, haven't burst into sobs.

Viera notices the color of my cheeks fading away, because she sits back against the wall of the chamber and laughs. "Nice work Empress. Good to know you can handle your spices."

I open my mouth to answer, but it's too dry, too torched to form any words so I close it again and swallow. Then we both hear noise from the entrance. Footsteps approaching.

My quartet of Shadows stands outside, as ever, though the persons involved rotate in shifts. Even so, I'm not afraid. Anything that could best the four of them, would only get through to Viera and her fire-spitting pistol. Past that, I have my own small version, special made for me, stored in a small box at my side. A knife beneath my robe, tied around my waist on a cotton belt. Plenty of options.

I don't have to use any of them, because it's Malo that appears, still sporting the lion's mane, and pulling another groveling man with him.

"My Empress," Malo drops into a quick bow. "This one approached Damantum's gates not long ago. He claims he's from the jungle. From the Solare and that he's run all night to get here."

"A far journey," I say. "One I don't think is possible?"

When I traveled here with Malo, it took a week to make it from my village to Damantum. Hard marching during the daylight hours. That one man could make the same trek in two days?

"Tell her," Malo shakes the man with his hand. Then releases him.

The Solare tribesman falls to the ground, places his palms flat against the stones, and his forehead follows them. He speaks into the ground. "My Empress, I came not from the jungle. I am the tenth in the string. Together, we relayed the message along the route you yourself created."

"I created?" I ask.

Malo coughs. I look at him. "Kaishi, when you ordered us to keep up better communications with Solare and the surrounding towns, we developed a system of runners. Like this one. They're stationed all over Charre, stretching to the jungle east and to the cities west and north, so that as soon as one receives notice they run to the next station, ensuring rapid delivery of critical information."

"You could've led with that," I say.

"Sorry," Malo says. "The man's message muddled my mind."

"Then let him speak it." Viera waves a hand with fish in it, one she shoves into her mouth a second later. I notice there are far fewer peppers on her portion than mine.

The runner starts speaking to the ground again and Malo pulls him up. "Speak directly to the Empress."

The man's eyes dart to Malo, then back to me. I nod, give him a small smile. I've learned that the smallest gestures of kindness can make all the difference in keeping someone loyal. Appreciative. Helpful.

"I can only tell you what I've been told," the man blubbers. "They're saying that more gods have come, Empress. Strange creatures taller than any of us. Four arms and tails. They talk in our tongue." At Malo's look, the man revises. "I mean, the Solare tongue."

"You mean the Lunare," Viera interjects.

"Viera," I warn. The woman has a love of conflict, and I don't have the patience for it right now.

The Charre speak a different version of my home language, one that both the jungle Solare and mountainous Lunare adopted. Trade urges fluency in both, though I've noticed most Charre, including Malo, learn the barest minimum of their partner tongue.

"Keep going," Malo says.

The man inclines his head. "These new gods say they're looking for someone who approached a crashed—" here the man stumbles over a word, then figures it out: "ship. Someone who speaks of magic and miracles."

The man doesn't say it, but we're all thinking it. Me.

I know what this is. Who they are.

I wave away the man. Thank him for the message. Malo escorts him outside, then returns. Returns in time for me to relay what Ignos just spewed into my mind.

They're invaders. From another world. My enemies and the enemies of all you and your people stand for. They will destroy everything to get to you, to me.

I deliver those words to Malo and Viera, then relay Ignos' commands. When I say we're supposed to gather our forces, march, and eliminate them, neither Viera nor Malo seem particularly perturbed at the thought of war, but they're fighters, so why would they be?

"To be honest, Empress," Viera says. "It's been getting a little dull in the city. I love it, but I was thinking I might take another trip to the Pits soon so I don't lose my edge."

"You talk about life and death is if it's a game," Malo says to the Lunare, who sighs as soon as the Charre starts talking. "Every fight should be fought with honor. Dedication. If we must pull men from their families and send them forth, the men must know what we are after. What their sacrifice is for. Then, when we claim our victory, our soldiers can sing of their triumph for seasons." Then Malo shrugs. "It will help us gather volunteers."

"It won't be the size of our force that matters," I say. "But the skill. A small band of our most talented, fearsome fighters. Ones that can fire an arrow with pinpoint accuracy, or slip through the thickest trees without being noticed. Ignos thinks there will only be two of them, though each is worth a hundred of our own."

"A hundred?" This is the first time Malo looks surprised, and I detect a bit of eagerness too. "Then we will take four hundred of our best, and hope that is enough."

"Send the messages, and inform the armorers; we'll need more weapons." I stand, the food suddenly tasting dry in my mouth.

I follow Malo outside chamber, and as he leaves and descends to start the preparations, I climb up. To the very top of the Vaos. I can see Nomis in her shimmering silver hovering over the fiery, beautiful carpet that is Damantum at night. It's a wonder. One I don't want to lose.

I ask Ignos if we'll be okay.

There's no answer.

6 / MISDIRECTION

Sax readies to break for the tree line when one of the singers comes forward from the cluster. This one looks older, at least by the conventional way such things are judged. There's gray in his hair, his skin bears the marks of both battle and age. But his eyes are vigorous. His mouth is tight.

"Our chieftain," says the guard who brought them here, and he sinks down to one knee.

Sax and Bas do not.

"We are looking for someone," Sax hisses as the chieftain nears.

He's at least two meters smaller than the Oratus. Frail. Easy to break. It's clear this species does not elect their leaders by strength alone. Perhaps they are not as primitive as they appear.

"Someone who changed," Bas continues for him. "Someone who may have talked of strange things. Of other places, of miracles and magic."

Both Sax and Bas know these words, and know this speech. This is far from the first world, or the first species to be discovered in the process of eradicating the Sevora. Once the Sevora became known, the Oratus and others worked to spread as quickly as possible throughout the galaxy. To uncover as many places and intelligent species as they could and bring them into the galactic fold.

This did not always work. Some, too shocked by the appearance of such advanced weaponry, species, and ships, simply failed to adapt. Either slaughtered each other, or lost their own ways and became gears ground in the established order of the galaxy. Their cultures died, and all things that made them unique vanished in their assimilation.

Even that, though, is better than serving the Sevora.

Sax watches as Bas talks. The person shows the signs: there's not enough surprise, not enough shock. Not only at what Bas is saying, but at the Oratus themselves. Creatures four meters high, with four arms and two legs ending in three large claws apiece. Long tails and heads, with mouths full of sharp teeth. Sax's appearance alone should send these people running. That it does not means they have seen or heard fantastical things.

This tribe, this village knows.

"I have heard such talk before," the chieftain replies slowly. "It came from there." He points behind them, to the jungle and towards the place where the seed crashed. "And it left soon after."

"These words do not leave on their own," Sax hisses. "We need to find who carries it."

The chieftain tilts his head. "You need to find a god?"

Sax can't help it. He hisses with laughter. It's clear the village, these humans don't quite know what's going on. The chieftain backpedals a step, and the guard kneeling next to Sax jerks up, spear tight.

"That, humans, is an Oratus laugh," Bas says, and now she hisses of her own accord. "What my pair means to say, is that what you saw is no god. A species playing tricks. Trying to turn you and your entire world into slaves for its own ends."

The chieftain shakes his head. "It wasn't a creature like you. The words came from the mouth of a girl. My own daughter."

Sax nods. The thing seems to understand the gesture. Good.

"The Sevora take over the minds of those they capture. They look and sound like the ones you know and love, but they are not." Sax points to one of the cooking animals, turning on a spit over one of the fires. "Your daughter is like that creature there. An animal, roasting and waiting as a Sevora eats her life."

Bas hisses a chiding sound. A warning not to be too dramatic. To scare or anger these people.

The chieftain only looks sad. "How are we to trust you? You tell us that my daughter is taken by something like that." He points to the meat. Not quite what Sax had intended, but no matter. "You tell me, strange beings, that we should trust you. That we should give you answers. Why?"

Sax glances at his claws, slowly enough that it's clear to everyone what he's doing. "Because this creature must be destroyed. Because it is a threat, not only to you in your world, but to all the others."

Once again, the words fail to faze the chieftain.

"Your daughter," Bas says. She's better with these sorts of connections. "You say she spoke of a god?"

"She didn't speak of a god," he replies. "She was. She is. Ignos is within her."

Bas is about to reply, Sax is staring at his claws as they shine in the firelight. They're sharp, ready.

"Then we will take him out." Bas says.

7 / TRAINING

Malo stands across from me, about ten paces away, with his arms crossed and a sardonic grin on his face.

"You're using that one again?" Malo says as his eyes track to my right hand and what I'm holding in it.

"It's the only one I'm good at," I say, though that's not strictly true.

I have managed to fire one of the guns, as we've taken to calling Ignos' miracles. I even hit the target.

The shard, though, has a more immediate feel to it. There's a weight, as I hold onto the rope grip, that the guns lack. Knowing that when I swing my arms, the interlinking glass shards will whip forward and slice anything in their way gives the shard a familiar feel. It's a weapon I can understand. One I can know.

It's an inferior tool. One you'll need to discard when the time comes.

Ignos thinks most of my choices are inferior, so his judgment doesn't bother me much. Instead, I square my shoulders to Malo, take one glance up at Nomis rising silver behind him, and settle into a slight squat. We've been working on positioning—keeping my knees from locking, resting on the balls of my feet, ready to shove off in any direction.

Malo doesn't move. Stands there. Meets my stare.

"I'm ready," I prompt, but he doesn't shift.

He's waiting for you.

I see that now. The only weapons Malo has are attached to his belt; short wooden staves with vicious, sharp talons curling away from the tops. Kukri. The shard has a meter or more of reach on those things, so I take a slow step forward, then snap my wrist.

The shard slides up from the ground, blowing sand as it moves and curls towards Malo's face. Only after I make the move does it occur to me that I could kill my army's leader, and my friend. But Malo slides back a step, turns to the side, and all the surprise attack gets me is the tiniest of cuts on Malo's left shoulder. He keeps his arms crossed. Waits for my next attack.

"I don't want to hurt you." I let the shard settle back into the sand, then pull it back towards me.

"That is my problem, not yours," Malo replies. "What did you do wrong there?"

"I almost had you."

"Almost. What did you do wrong?"

I think, but I'm suddenly irritated. Malo should be focusing on the fact that I nearly shredded his arm off, not asking me questions. I'm about to bark that idea at him, when I see that he's not kidding.

There's a set to his face, to his body, still turned to its side, that says answering this question might be the key between my living or dying some day.

"I was too slow?"

"You were too direct." Malo faces me again, kicks at the sand. "Every move you made led right to the attack you planned. In a real fight, you cannot give yourself away. Feint, then come at me again."

"Won't you know I'm feinting?"

"Not if you do it right."

I take a deep breath. Look to my right, where the campfires of my army make a glittering constellation on the dark sand. To my left, where the valley wall begins to rise into a rocky brown cliff. Above, starlight peeks between a rare cloud drift, racing to catch Nomis' glow.

"I'm done for tonight," I say, loosening my grip.

I head towards the fire, making a quarter turn right and taking steps, the shard dragging in the sand behind me.

"We've only just started," Malo says, and I hear him catch up with me.

At his third step, I whirl. This time, I use my body, along with my arm, to whip the shard around. Its glinting blades slice through the air in an arc, whistling as I spin around. I get to see Malo's eyes go wide, see him fall and land on his back in the dirt as the shard whistles above. He and I both know that, in a real fight, I could crack the weapon back and send it slinging down towards him before the Charre warrior would have a chance to move.

"Surprise you that time?" I say.

Malo sits up slow, gives me a nod. "Much better. Though I would not expect that trick to work on just anyone."

"Only on you."

It's what I might have said, but Viera gets there first. She's striding towards us, and by the way she's shaking her head at Malo, it's clear she's seen what happened.

"The Empress alone has that advantage," Malo replies, starting to stand up from the sand.

"Does she?" Viera says. "Do you know why the Lunare win most of our fights, Malo?"

"Because your kind doesn't care about honor."

"Exactly."

"Now you're both annoying me," I interrupt. "Viera, what are you doing here?"

"Food's ready, Empress," Viera looks over at me "Didn't want it to get cold while you're out here playing in the sand."

"Training." Malo joins us. "There may yet come a time when neither of us can defend her, and Kaishi must fight for herself."

"With that?" Viera looks at the shard with the same skepticism Malo showed moments ago.

"I like it," I say again. "It's effective."

"You want effective, try these," Viera pats her pistols. "Instant gratification. No need to get up close. Especially when your enemy has breath like this guy here."

Malo sighs, then looks to me, "Tomorrow, Empress, I'd like to revisit this. Viera has a point—you must be able to feint away an adversary, not only your teacher." He brushes by us before Viera can come up with another insult.

"Why are you so hard on him?" I say to Viera as we watch the warrior go.

"Hard on him? Malo doesn't care what I say."

"I think you're wrong." I put my hand on Viera's shoulder, to forestall her opening mouth. "I'd like both my friends to stop behaving like enemies. If Ignos is right, if what we're up against is as terrible as he's telling me, we'll all need to work together."

"If Ignos is right, Empress, it might not matter."

8 / THE LUNARE

Dawn finds both Sax and Bas tired. They slept through the night in shifts, one for four hours and the other the next.

Not that an Oratus needs a full night's rest to feel relaxed, but a little bit helps. The morning meal, full of the meat the chieftain labels pork, wakes them up somewhat. Followed by a warm drink of something called tea; a watery, herbal liquid that nonetheless kicks some part of Sax's brain into overdrive.

Then the young warrior that found them in the forest the previous night approaches, says he'll be the one to lead them east. Towards where the chieftain's daughter went.

In the bright daytime, the jungle is colorful. Full of moving animals and birds. Plants twisting in the breeze. Buzzing insects that find themselves unable to get through the masks both Bas and Sax wear, and the two draw jealous glances from the warrior, whose covered himself in sticky, smelly sap that's nowhere close to equaling a mask's proficiency.

They step across ferns and vines, and trails barely visible until they are already upon them. At one point they hop over a series of stones to cross the shallow river.

Neither Bas nor Sax speak much during the journey. He's

absorbing information, keeping an eye out for hazards. Bas is likely doing the same. There's no reason to waste words.

It's not until evening, with the young man never tiring, that they reach the foothills and the first sign of civilized life they've seen in a while. A hardened, deep-wood wall, appearing at the end of the trail with a wide gate, that extends as far as Sax and Bas can see through the crowded, foliage-filled space.

On top of the wall, as the planet's star slides towards setting, a pair of pale-skinned guards look down at them. Unlike their guide, who wears a simple mosswrap, these two wear deep green tunics, cotton clothes. Thicker than necessary, and it shows, based on the sweat that coats their faces.

"What horrors are you?" one of the guards shouts.

The other one says nothing but aims a wide-ended gray-metal tube their way. A primitive gun, though far beyond what they saw at the small village. Its presence is a sign the Sevora is here. A sign that the Sevora's influence is already spreading. The parasite is moving fast.

"They seek an audience with your leader," their guide shouts. "They came to our jungle last night, and so we brought them to you."

"With Avril? What gives them the right?"

Sax looks at the man. He's the same as the other members of their species. Soft, simple. And, Sax has no doubt, easily intimidated. He punches his legs and leaps. High up to the very top of the gate, where he digs his claws into the wood and clamors over. Now he towers over the one who'd asked the question.

Staring down at him, Sax opens his mouth ever so slightly, just enough to give a sure glimpse of all the teeth inside.

Sax senses the other guard aiming his gun and cocking its hammer, and Sax whips his tail. Knocks the weapon from the man's hand and sends it flying.

"We seek an audience with your leader because we want one," Sax hisses. "This Avril will meet us, or they will die. Along with all of you."

The man's look slides from Sax's face to his left. Sax follows. On the other side of the wall is a sprawling tent town. Simple fortifications. Small buildings made of wood and cloth. Not a long-term settlement. A military camp. There are plenty of soldiers, staring up at them. Some are fishing for their own guns, but Sax isn't worried. Even if the bullets could pierce the mask, which Sax doesn't think they can, a few quick shots of his own miner would doubtless render them petrified.

"I can tell her," the guard stammers. "I can send the communication. If it's agreed, we'll let you in. Take you to Avril."

"You will take us to her now," Sax hisses. "She will not refuse."

The man goes even paler, to a shade of white Sax is not used to seeing in the living.

There's a bump, a scratching as Bas climbs herself over the wall. As she picks up the other guard and holds him aloft, off the ledge.

"We will speak to your leader, and we will do you no harm," Bas roars out to the assembling crowd. "If you attempt to hurt us, attack us in any way, we will slaughter all of you. And we will enjoy it."

That last seems to do the trick. Guns drop. Swords return to sheaths. Just like that, the two Oratus have themselves a captured force.

"Where is she?" Sax asks the guard he's still holding in his claws.

"In our capital, of course," the man says. "Marilo, deep inside the mountains."

"Then you will lead us there. Now."

9 / HOMECOMING

It has only been months. A single whole season gone. Yet home feels like another world to me. I see the Tier, standing only a fourth as high as the Vaos and infinitely smaller in width and grandeur. I see our stone houses, which felt so large to my old self and now seem as though they could all fit within a single Damantum courtyard. All of my childhood compressed into a fraction of the empire I now rule.

Whatever remains of the girl that left this village dies when I see Father.

When I last left him, he had looked down on me from the Tier. Watched, along with the rest of my village as I had gathered up my meager pack, my mosswrap and marched away with the Charre soldiers—Malo included—from my home.

Now he sees me at the head of great force. Sees me dressed in fine robes, with emeralds hanging from my ears and neck, wearing more on my body than the worth of his entire village. Father doesn't see his daughter anymore. That much is clear.

You have grown beyond him.

I wince at Ignos' words. There's a difference between knowing something and having it told to you. Father, and Mother beside him, lead a small band of our village's hunters; faces I recognize. People who once asked me to do errands, who ran with me through the trees during games. Now they stare at me with guarded faces, hidden souls.

They walk towards me as I stand on the edge of the clearing, with Malo and Viera by my side and several hundred Charre warriors at my back. Common Solare respect dictates a visitor should not enter a village without the permission of its elders, and, despite the ability of my army to raze my home a dozen times over, I hold true to that custom.

"Kaishi," Father says as he comes up to me. I see a flash of recognition as he notices Viera at my side—the Lunare had been trading in our village prior to Malo's arrival—but I cut off any further words.

I step forward, wrap my arms around Father, and pull him in tight. Release and do the same for Mother, who, I notice, enters into the embrace more willingly. She is only hugging her daughter, whereas Father hugs the leader of a rival empire. When I stand back, though, I notice both of them can't resist small smiles. Their simmering happiness warms my heart more than anything.

"They were here," Father continues, guessing at why I've come.

"Who were they?"

"*What* were they is the better question," Father replies, and I hear a cascade of murmurs make their way through the village hunters behind him.

Murmurs that only grow louder as Father describes a pair of monsters, taller than any man and with four arms, a tail, and claws as long as Malo's kukri blade.

"But they are no longer here," Malo states as Father concludes his description.

"We sent them away. To the East." Father can't resist looking at Viera.

"You sent them to my people," Viera says. "Of course. Why not, when confronted with devastation, pass it on to somebody else?"

"Better our enemies than ourselves," Father replies.

"Then we will follow them," I say, trying to keep Viera in check. "Either we'll catch them before they reach the mountains, or we'll help the Lunare fight them off. It might even be a chance for our two empires to come together."

Perhaps, with both of your armies working together, you might win.

"Two empires?" Father asks.

The Charre, the Solare, and the Lunare. Three peoples, with the Solare stuck between more powerful neighbors. No one, Father included, could believe the Solare would survive should either the Charre or Lunare let the other have the jungle. Mutual fear keeps my old village alive. Ignos has been telling me the time for that is at an end—I have his guidance, and I should bring the Solare and their resources into my widening grip.

"It will be better, father," I say slowly, measuring his reaction to every word. "With Charre resources and the miracles Ignos provides, the Solare will be happier. Healthier. There will be no more fear."

"You would rule over us?" Father asks, and his voice is innocent.

Careful.

I don't need Ignos to warn me. This man is my father. I've had a thousand arguments with him, watched as he dismantled the verbal parries of a hundred traders and visitors from other villages. Getting into a war of words with him is a choice I do not want to make. So I stop the fight before it can start.

"I *am* ruling over you," I say. "As your daughter, and your empress. When we turned back the Lunare, the tribes with them pledged their loyalty to me. As have the Charre people."

"As we have not." Father stands straighter.

"As you will do, now." I push hard iron into my voice.

The jungle goes still for a long moment.

"You know we cannot resist you, Kaishi," Father says finally, waving his arm back at the village behind him. "We are small, simple. All we have is our independence. The right to determine for ourselves what is right."

Which has brought them nowhere. You will make them better. You will make the world better, with my help.

"When the Lunare come again, what will happen?" I say. "Whose daughter will you give up next time to send them away?"

I can see those words hurt. My parents do not meet my eyes. Even Malo, the hardened warrior who took me from this place, glides a concerned glance my way. I don't back down. Don't look away.

"There is no other choice, Father," I continue. "You will join, as will all the other Solare. Together, we will make a better world."

He's not giving in. I see him put a hand on Mother's shoulder, and I know what's coming next.

I came here to help Father, not kill him. So I speak first.

"You told me, when I left, not to resist. Told me that everyone here would suffer if I did," I speak softly, so that those behind Father have to strain to hear. "I'm telling you the same thing now. Join me, help me find the monsters who came here, and save your village. Save our people."

My words douse the fire in his eyes, and once his spark is out, Father nods. For the first time in months, his hands clasp mine, but I feel no love in their grip, only sadness.

They will understand, Kaishi, when you deliver them from their harsh existence. They will love you for it.

I hope, but I don't believe.

10 / INTO DARKNESS

Ten humans guide them through the caves. Five in front and five behind. A ratio Sax is comfortable with, as the narrow caverns mean his tail alone could knock all trailing him to the ground while his claws deal with those ahead. Bas being beside him only means any attempt at resistance would be so futile, so useless as to be unimaginable.

Which the stance of their guards, their low shoulders and huffing, nervous breath conveys. Their fear fills the air, mingling with the cool, rusted scent of mineral water coming from the stream sharing their path. The trickle coats the stones on their right, occasionally pooling and then rushing onward again, further and further down.

The state of this world and the creatures on it leads Sax to expect darkness, and he's ready to switch his mask to an infrared spectrum as they descend past the point of daylight. Until he notices glows, of a blue and purple cast, coming ahead of them. The guards make no mention of this, but keep trudging forward. Sax refuses to ask questions, and his patience is answered seconds later when the source comes into view.

Mushrooms and moss, glowing on the rocks in patches. The stalks shimmer blue as they rise from the ground, from cracks in the stone or from the patches of dirt mingling in the crannies. The moss clings to the ceiling, a phosphorescent pink, its shine bright enough to give some idea of where they're going, if still too dim to lay out the path as clear as day.

"Cultivated?" Sax says to the guard leading them, the one he took hold of on the wall, as they pad along.

"Throughout Lunare, yes," the guard replies, a bit of pride making itself known. "They're the only way we get light down here, short of torches. You'd be surprised how many sticks you've got to burn to keep an empire lit."

"So you plant these things along your routes."

"Living beneath the rock doesn't come naturally." As if to illustrate the point, the guard steps carefully around what looks like rubble from a fallen boulder. "Takes being clever, takes having the guts to deal with problems instead of hoping they'll get better. It's why the surface tribes can't handle us."

"If they can't handle you, then why are you still here?"

Bas touches his tail again, but Sax ignores his pair this time. If they're marching into a dangerous place, to confront dangerous people and demand the head of their leader, Sax wants to know all about them. What keeps these people going, what they're afraid of, and why they choose to live outside the light.

The cave breaks into a wide chamber, split in half by the creek, and thick stalagmites and stalactites rise from floor and ceiling like alien sculptures. Patches of the moss and mushrooms give the place a surreal radiance, and for a moment Sax feels like he's back aboard the seed ship, stuck in that nightmare world of flashing entertainment, where the parasites could forget the lives they stole from those who deserved them.

"Hard to leave home, I suppose," the guard says as they crunch through the room. "It's not like they've got it better up there anyway. Have to deal with storms, lots of bugs, dangerous animals. Down here it's quiet, and in the cities, always warm. Just saying that if we wanted to, we could take them."

Not if they attacked as poorly as they defended, but Sax doesn't say that. They're far from their shuttle now, and neither he nor Bas has any idea how these tunnels go together. If their guards decided to run away, the two Oratus would have a hard time finding their way anywhere.

"How long have you been here?" Sax asks. "How many cycles?"

"Cycles?"

They speak galactic common, but don't know about cycles? One tribe uses the most primitive spears, bows and arrows, while this one wields guns. The variances here are confusing. Nonsensical. Unless someone outside intervened.

"A standard length of time," Bas is explaining. "Cycles are marked by major events. Like the defeat of the Sevora, or the colonizing of a new system."

"I don't understand the words you're using," the guard replies. "But the Lunare have been in these mountains longer than I've been alive, my father and his father too. Longer than that, I'd imagine."

Long enough for natural evolution? Sax isn't a biologist, but there are certain trends between species in the galaxy; the Flaum have big eyes, furry coats and small bodies because they lived, originally, on a cratered world with little light. Cold, with meager food supplies. Couldn't have been too unlike these caves, yet the people walking the Oratus through these underground pathways, aside from their pale skin, look unsuited to a place like this.

Sax turns these thoughts over in his mind as they trudge along through more, and narrower, passages until they again open up into a chamber. This one, though, is far larger than the first. So big that Sax can't see the ceiling, the far wall. So big that it contains houses, streets, a whole town lit in blues and pinks from mushrooms and moss.

"You think this is big?" the guard laughs, looking at the two of them. "Gove is an outpost, nothing more. A spot to rest before we head on to Marilo tomorrow."

There's noise coming from the village, the sound of drills turning and hammers pounding. Smells of soot and cookfires cling to the wet air, and Sax notes the creek seems to run right through the center of the town. They continue on an avenue alongside it, and Sax is very aware of pressing eyes on him as they move. Their claws are causing a panic throughout, Sax is sure.

Gove's center consists of a rounded courtyard split in two by the creek. Twin walking bridges, with silvery rails over gray stone arches, connect the two halves. On either side is a cut geode, the two broken edges facing each other from across the water, made to stand on small pedestals.

Storefronts, with those mushrooms glowing in the windows, call out offerings for shelter, for mining gear and food. Yet there seems to be nobody here aside from the ten of them. Even the sounds of hammers and drills die away as the group of them move into the courtyard's center.

When the guard stops near the geode, when the other nine with him fan out around Sax and Bas, the Oratus already know what's about to happen. Their claws are ready. Their tails swish. These Lunare are about to make a fatal mistake.

"Looks like you two don't know caves," the guard says. "We've had runners going ahead of us the whole way. Gove is ready for you."

The guard raises his right hand, and Sax notices the fear that had gripped the man on top of the wall is buttressed by confidence. Something's given his courage back.

When the rumblings come, a chorus of them that echo from the floors and ceilings, Sax understands. From each of the seven streets leading into the courtyard, white-furred beasts stride up, each one mounted by a pale-skinned creature. Eyeless, strange and monstrous, the Fassoths tower above their apparent masters.

These things shouldn't be here. Not on a world so far from populated space.

Yet, here they are, and the Oratus can do nothing except surrender.

11 / GOD'S CHARIOT

The object is unnatural. It sits between the trees, and on some of them, having crushed them to the ground in its gray bulk. Ignos tells me it's made of metal, and that it's pieced together part by part, which explains the thin lines running across it. Like scales, only squared and perfect. There's a bulb at the very front, with what looks like a transparent plate across it.

Glass. To see through, while providing protection.

I walk beneath the ship—what Ignos tells me it's called—and stare up. There's several meters between my head and the ship's bottom, and here I see the gray is scarred with black streaks. As if it's been burned. I see where the three struts, two in back and another in front, extend from the ship. The connections are large, circular.

Charre warriors, along with my old village's hunters, look at the ship with me. One had seen the craft some days ago. After the two creatures had arrived at my village, after Father had lied to send them away. Now I'm here, with Viera, Malo, and some of my force, to try and learn what we can about the new gods that have decided to visit our world.

Gods. It's not the name Ignos wants for them, but it's what the tribesmen say. What else, after all, could be so different? Could arrive in a craft so vastly unlike anything that we have?

I care about you. They do not. I will give you miracles. They will take your lives.

Good and evil don't determine what makes a god. I put my hand against the front strut, feel the metal and how hot it's getting in Ignos' light. The ship ruined the canopy here, and the light is so bright my left hand is ever-present above my eyes, shading them.

Doing that, I can see that the jungle isn't wasting any time in claiming the ship as its own; nests are forming in creases, bundles of leaves and branches. Ferns and vines are making tentative forays up the struts from the ground, wrapping around the ship's feet.

It's been here for some time already. Well more than a week.

"Kaishi," Malo says, joining me beneath the front bulb. "Can Ignos tell us what's inside? Or how to get there?"

I can't. This is not a door I can open for you.

At my shaking head, Malo sighs. "All this adds, then, is questions."

"It answers one," I say, and Malo waits for me to continue. "Why they came here. Look."

I point to the remnants of the crashed seed, the hole where I found Ignos so long ago.

"They didn't choose this place randomly." I walk to the edge of the pit. Push back encroaching memories, the moment when I couldn't feel my arms and legs, the sucking black ink. "They wanted this seed. They want Ignos."

"We knew they wanted you." Malo isn't impressed, apparently.

"But not me." I look down at myself. "At least, I don't think they want Kaishi. What they want is Ignos, the god inside of me."

Malo tilts his head. "Ignos is inside of you? Physically?"

"I don't know," I say. "When I met Ignos, I found one like this, but much smaller. Ignos says it was his. So he must have come inside of it, right?"

I did.

"Why would a god need to travel inside such a small ship?" Malo asks, then turns back to the larger, newer one. "If these gods come in something so much larger, then perhaps we really are in trouble."

"Father said there were two of them. Do you think we could lose to so few?"

Malo shakes his head. "A season ago, I would have said no. Now, with what we've seen, with what we've unleashed? I don't know, Kaishi. I don't know if we have any place with warring gods."

I nod. Ignos had implied much the same. Which makes what I say next easier.

"Malo, if they've come here for me, for Ignos, and we can't stop them?" Malo picks up the tone in my voice, pays close attention. "I'll let them take me. Make them promise to leave the rest of our people alone. Then we'll survive."

"But you will not."

"The Emperor, when we faced the Charre, rode out in front," I say, remembering. "He put himself before his army, his people, knowing the risks. Knowing that his sacrifice would be worth it. I can do the same."

Malo puts a hand on my shoulder. "Then, my Empress, we must not fail. We will drive these gods from our lands and make them understand that we are not their prey. You will return to your city a savior, and the world you and Ignos envision will come to pass."

His touch, his words make me smile. "I hope so, Malo. I do."

We stay at the ship a little longer, but can't find any way inside of it, so when Ignos slips down towards the horizon, I make the call to return to the village. In the morning we'll march again. To the East, through the rest of the jungle and towards the mountains. Towards the Lunare.

Towards war.

12 / AN INSPECTION

Seven Fassoths, and now seventeen guards. Sax estimates he and Bas could pull their weapons, down one or two of the large creatures with their miners before the others crushed them. Which would leave the Sevora free to continue its dominance.

No. A fight isn't the way. Sax loosens his muscles, moves his claws away from the bars clipped into his mask.

"You have us," Bas says, reading Sax's motions. "Though we never claimed we wanted to hurt you."

"It's not about what you claimed, but about what you are. I am Avril, and the Lunare you threaten are my people," the voice comes from the top of one of the buildings, and Sax notices, leaning over the flat roof, a female of the species. This is the first one he's seen with shock-white hair, with a face far paler than the rest. "Monsters, do you have names? Or should I think of you solely as nightmares?"

She's also the first one to look at them without fear.

"We are visitors," Sax hisses, and both of them give up their names. There's little risk in doing so—either this is the Sevora host, and they will all be dead shortly, or they are not, in which case the Oratus will leave and never return. "We are looking for a problem that chose to land on your world."

Sax and Bas perform an immediate assessment of Avril. The guards are paying her obvious deference, so she must be the leader. Yet, she hasn't ordered them killed, which any Sevora would do. Unless it's already started reproducing. Unless it means to capture the Oratus as well.

"I could argue that you are the problem," Avril says, not moving from her perch, and Sax sees a pair of shadows behind her. Other guards, most likely. "Didn't you disrupt my fortification outside the mountain? Haven't you forced my soldiers to take you here?"

"What we did is nothing compared to what will happen if you prevent us from completing our mission." Bas replies.

"Then persuade me. Now."

"Are you free?" Sax asks before Bas can say anything.

"Free?"

"Do you make your own choices? Are your people able to decide for themselves what to do with their lives?" Sax stays away from the irony in this, as he knows he has no such freedom for his own existence. Still, if he had a choice, Sax would choose to be right here.

Well, perhaps not right here, surrounded by death, but—

"I do. The Lunare do." Avril's curious now, relaxing.

"What we are seeking will change that. Will tear that freedom away and turn you into slaves. Husks made to serve its desires."

"If we met such a creature, we would destroy it."

"The Sevora do not stay in the open," Bas interrupts. "They slip inside your mind, they take you when you are not ready. They could be here, right now, and you would never know."

"They cannot be seen?"

"They live inside you." Sax scans the crowd as he says the words, and he sees the guards' eyes follow his.

Murmurs spring up, and uncertainty spreads. Questions leap to a dozen mouths and die, unasked, as Sax watches the guards assess their friends. Who among them might be one of this creature's pets?

"There must be some sign of this thing you seek," the woman says. "Or why would you be here searching for it?"

"A Sevora," Bas says. "First seeks to rebuild its own society. To create a world where its kind can flourish. You will know its presence by the sudden spark of genius. By the miraculous inventions of things unknown to your world."

These words strike the woman and her face slides into contemplation. It's a long moment before she speaks.

"Not long ago, a grand force of ours swept forth from these mountains intent on ending the constant strife that has plagued these lands. Warring tribes who never seem to tire of sending one another's children to the tops of altars. We prefer not to sacrifice our own, and thought to spread our more civilized ways. However, our force was stopped. Halted by an army with weapons they should not have had, beyond our own abilities. Weapons they did not have months ago."

"East of here?" Sax asks.

Avril shakes her head. "West. The Charre empire. Ruled now, I'm told, by a young priestess. One who, as you say, came to power with a string of miracles. Who promises much, and then delivers."

The village elder. The old man. Either he lied or Avril is lying now. A Sevora tactic. If Bas and Sax did as Avril is suggesting, if they left and went all the way back west, they would lose so much time. Enough for a Sevora to devise an escape, or develop more lethal tools.

"We can make you an offer," Sax says, and Avril waits, letting Sax continue. "Let us examine you. Find you clear of the Sevora. If you are, then we will leave and look for this priestess you mention."

"And if I am not?"

"Then you will not feel anything," Sax replies. "Your death will be swift, painless."

"Yours would not be," Avril says. "Kill me here and so many will descend upon you, my people will grind you into nothing."

"Then let's hope it doesn't come to that."

Avril takes the words without emotion, but vanishes from the rooftop. Moments later she pushes open the front door of one of the nearby shops. Strides towards Sax, who looks down at her with toothy determination.

"What is your test?" Avril asks.

"Stand still," Sax replies.

He reaches behind him and grasps a thin silver bar attached to the back of his mask. Takes it forward and holds it next to Avril's head.

The guards around them tense, and the Fassoths lean forward against their saddles, ready to charge at the slightest command. With his right foreclaw, Sax turns the silver bar so that it's level with Avril's left ear. She's staring at him now, close, and he can see that her eyes are a kind of pinkish-red. A fascinating color.

Sax moves the silver bar so that it touches the woman's ear, and then he presses in on a slight indent a third of the way up the device. It hums, a frequency too high for them to hear, but Sax feels the vibrations. A Sevora would feel them all down its many nerves, shaking and dislodging the creature, spurring it to escape the twinging agony.

Nothing happens, and Avril continues to stare at Sax until he pulls the bar away.

"Tell me more about this force to the West," Sax hisses, and the corners of Avril's mouth curl up into a smile.

13 / TWO FORCES

Several more marching days pass before the Lunare outpost's wooden walls fade in through the morning jungle fog. A barrier my force can easily pass by burning it down.

I hope we don't have to.

A pair of Lunare, standing atop the gate with their guns held ready, stare out at Viera, Malo and I as we approach. There's a chance they'll just shoot us, so a trio of Charre warriors, holding thick, long and wide shields, march in front. The cover isn't total, but makes the odds of a good shot low, and my line of archers with bows stretched and arrows ready ensures the Lunare would only get one off.

"We're here to talk," I shout, as the two guards say nothing at my approach.

"A lot of people just for talking!" the right guard replies.

"It's a dangerous subject," I say. "Where is the leader of this outpost?"

"Busy."

"You know who you're talking to?" Viera interrupts. "This is the Empress of the Charre. You'll treat her with respect, or I'll shoot you where you stand."

I'm at once annoyed and flattered by Viera's response. It's nice to know she cares, though I don't want a fight here if I can help it. I didn't bring the thousands upon thousands of warriors I'd need to assault the Lunare. It's a surgical force, with a single objective.

"I know perfectly well who I'm speaking to," the guard says. "And I'm not a part of the Charre Empire, so I'll talk to her as I damn well please."

"Viera," I say quietly, firmly. "Leave this to me."

I'm a little surprised when, with a slight bow of her head, my friend acquiesces and keeps her mouth shut. I take a breath, look back to the guard, who's now wearing a stupid grin. Like he's won a fight.

"Two things may have come this way," I begin. "They would have looked strange to you. Unlike anything you've ever seen. They were searching for me."

They've been here. The guards are giving it away with their glances. Even I catch the quick flash between the guards, a moment of blinked congress to decide how to respond. That they aren't clueless or confused tells me all I need to know.

"We've seen what you're talking about. Two of'em. Mean-looking monsters." The guard points over his shoulder, towards the mountain rising up behind the outpost. "We're leading them into Lunare right now. They wanted a chat with our own leader, Avril."

"A chat?" I ask.

"Don't know if it's going to be more than that," the guard says. "Point being, they're on the other side of these walls, which is a place you won't be seeing anytime soon. I'd take your army and go home if I was you."

I have two options: I can order an assault, attack the wall and, maybe, win. I'd lose men, but we prepared for this last night. Or I can back off. Wait to see what happens.

They are here for you. For me. Whatever they find in that mountain won't be what they're looking for. We do know, though, that they'll come back once they know you're here. We can use that. Prepare.

"Can you carry a message for me? From the Charre Empress?" I say to the guard, who shrugs. "To Avril, or to those creatures, if they can be found. Let them know that I'm here waiting for them."

"You want to stick your army in the muddy jungle, be our guest," the guard says. "I'll send your word along, and when those things tear you apart, we'll come right behind. Take what ought to be ours anyway."

I'm tempted to raise my hand. Let the arrows fly. But an Empress can't give into temptation. She has to think about her people first. That's what Father did, and that's what I do now when I order our band back—the three warriors holding the shields raise them up, casting shade over my back.

"You mean to have us wait?" Malo says as soon as we're under the cover of the trees. "Sit here while the Lunare plan an ambush, or a full-scale assault?"

"We can't march back, Malo," I reply. "Have our warriors set up camp. Start cooking fires. And rig defenses."

"So you do expect a fight here," Viera says, and she doesn't look too disappointed by the idea.

"Ignos thinks these creatures will pursue us regardless. So yes, once they realize the Lunare don't have what they're looking for, I think they'll come for me."

"Which is why we should return to Damantum," Malo argues. "There we have strong walls and thousands who will fight for you. Coming this far was a mistake."

"Thousands who will die for me, Malo." I lean against a tree, its cool bark something I've felt too little of in my months with the Charre. "I can't take the chance these things would destroy Damantum to get to me."

"I think she's made her choice, lion man." Viera moves next to me and matches my stare towards Malo, who flicks his eyes at Viera.

"Kaishi, you asked me to lead your guards. Your armies," Malo's talking evenly now, the tone that says he wants my close attention, "I'm not the most experienced warrior we have, nor the most brilliant general among your ranks, so I can only believe you put me here because you trust what I have to say."

"Because you're my friend," I reply.

"Then listen to me now." Malo points back towards the Lunare outpost. "They are not going to sit while a Charre force rests outside their borders. We will wait for these creatures, and while we do, the Lunare will prepare an attack of their own. In one strike, they'll eliminate all of us, and our country will be left without its leaders. It's a dangerous mistake to stay."

The Oratus, the things that are after you, will not wait. Once they know that you are here, they will come, whether these Lunare are ready to follow them or not.

"Ignos says the creatures will come for us quick," I say. "We prepare, and we'll wait here for two days. After that time, if the creatures haven't made their strike, we'll retreat."

It's not what Malo wants to hear, but I'm still the Empress. I'm still his leader, and the lion warrior does not defy me. Malo turns away, shouts the commands, and my band bursts into activity.

My right hand lingers on top of the shard's handle, and I wait for death to come to me.

14 / DEADLY DESIGNS

Daylight is far brighter after a long time spent underground. It only takes a moment for the mask to adjust the filters for Sax, shading his vision and allowing him to see down the front of the mountainside clearly, where the arrayed Lunare forces wait behind their wooden wall. Several Fassoths stand amongst the guards, hitched with thick ropes to towers that sit on large rolling wheels. Lunare soldiers clamber around on them, taking up positions, as if they expect an attack will come at any moment.

"The enemy is waiting right beyond our walls," Avril explains as she notices Sax and Bas watching. The Lunare leader journeyed back with them, and she's peppered them with questions every moment of the way.

At first, Sax splintered in some of his own, interjections about Lunare culture and methods, how they grew and developed under the mountains. Avril's answers, though, proved unsatisfying. Vague and full of unknowns, though Sax figures that her wandering explanations are as much because Avril lacks the knowledge as any desire to mislead the Oratus.

What continues to be clear, though, is that the Sevora have no place in Lunare society. None of the methods, the systems employed by these cave-dwelling people match what Sax sees in the parasites. They're clean, even if the presence of things like the Fassoths strikes Sax as strange.

When Avril took over the questioning, though, it became Sax's turn to evade. She wanted technical descriptions, blueprints and instructions for how to create the masks, the miners, for how to surf the stars as the Oratus do. Sax gave her only the vaguest ideas, the loosest sketches.

Bas contributed silence. It's not the job of the Oratus to bring new species into the galactic fold.

"Will they attack?" Sax asks Avril. "The enemy?"

"I'm told they've set up their encampment out of range, but close. Put up minor fortifications. They wouldn't bother with that if the Charre were going to move against us soon."

"So they're setting a trap."

"I wouldn't call it a trap," Avril says. "They're waiting for you. They respect you."

"How many?"

"Several hundred. It's not a large force."

Avril doesn't say it, but her answer makes it clear: these Charre have come only for the Oratus. To take Sax and Bas and end their threat. And the only reason they would know the Oratus are threats is if a Sevora told them.

"We will strike tonight," Sax says.

"Do you need support?"

Sax is about to say no, but Bas beats him to it, "We do not need anything, but, if you are prepared to offer it, distraction would make it easier."

"I think we can provide some." Avril points at the mobile towers. "They have cannons. Loud, large, and perfect at getting attention."

They're almost down the mountain path now, stomping along the gravel rock. Ignos drifts in its afternoon descent, and clouds are chasing after it, promising rain. Better cover for their assault.

"Avril," Sax tries the name, but the hissing mangles it. "Why are you helping us?"

"Because without their empress, the Charre will fall."

Sax pauses, surprised at the lack of deception. No attempt to disguise her naked ambitions. Then again, Sax doesn't care what happens on this planet, or to this species. What's important is that the Sevora do not gain control.

"Does that worry you?" Avril asks, seeing Sax's hesitation.

"My mission has nothing to do with your power struggles," Sax says. "So long as we find the Sevora, nothing else matters."

Rain and darkness both fall soon after, with the clashing bangs of thunder and lancing bolts of lightning joining in. Sax and Bas assemble at the head of the Lunare force—with Avril watching from atop the wooden wall. It's a quick check to make sure both of them, freshly fed on fungal soups and jungle creature meat, are ready; masks tuned to lowlight vision, miners charged and operational, stim vials at hand if necessary.

Sax lifts his right foreclaw towards Avril, who lifts her right hand in response. Then the two Oratus leap. First, up to Avril's level. As they crouch, ready to scramble over, Sax hears Avril say, "Good luck, gods. I hope you find what you came for, and I hope I never see you again."

"Agreed," Sax hisses back, and then they're over the wall.

Both Sax and Bas catch the ground in a squat, then burst to the left. Out of the main pathway and into the trees. They don't go far before scaling a pair of thick-trunked, leafy ones. Climb all the way to the top, where the two of them poke out above the canopy, where the wind and rain pelt their masks.

From here they can see, even in this storm, the spotted orange glows of fires. At ground level, beneath the canopy, enough of the pouring water is blocked to allow such things. Not that Sax is complaining—a clear path to their target is all he can ask for.

Together, the two of them lope from one tree to the next, timing their leaps to coincide with cracks of lightning and the loud thundering rumbles. It's slow-going, but Avril asked for time to get those massive things moving, and it's better for the Oratus if they're not seen.

But these humans are not fools. Or the Sevora have instructed them well, as before long Sax leaps onto another tree and nearly winds up landing on one of them. The warrior is covered with bark and grime, though the rain washes it off in streaks. Still, in the night, he's mostly invisible, and Sax only realizes he's there when the warrior gives a shocked yelp.

Sax is on a thick branch, and his tail is already wrapping around the tree's trunk, a way of stabilizing him should the branch crack. Less than a meter away, on a second branch, crouches the human, already recovering from his shock and swinging his small bow and arrow to bear. Sax doesn't have time to pull a weapon, so instead he leans forward, towards the tree, and bites through the branch holding the man. Oratus teeth can cut metal, and the wood shreds like fluff in the face of those razors.

The man vanishes, crashing all the way down to the jungle floor. He might live, but when Sax watches for motion, blocks out the rain and focuses the mask on the body, there's no sound.

"They have scouts in the trees," Sax says, the mask linking him with Bas and sending the words to her.

"Did you see one?"

"I did. He fell."

Bas' hissing laugh comes through the mask, and Sax can't help but join. Quietly, though.

Then it's on to the next tree.

Eventually, sputtering fires spread beneath them. Clusters of warriors, dressed more simply and sparsely than the Lunare, huddle around the flames. Lean-tos and small tents covered with animal skins dot the area, the little concession to shelter here. As Avril said, this is a camp, but it's not a settlement. Nothing here is made to last.

It's not hard to spot the quartet of guards in front of one fire farther apart than the others. The four stand at taut attention, with spears in their hands, looking outward. Even upward, but Sax and Bas—who is high up in a tree five meters away from her pair—are too far away to see in the dark. To Sax, the guards appear as bright green forms, and behind them, kneeling around the fire, are two others.

One is smaller than the other creatures. Avril and the other Lunare suggested the Sevora host is young. This size would fit.

A rolling rumble of thunder is followed, moments later, by a louder, more direct bang. Something breaks through the trees far to Sax's right; the Lunare plan to fire wide of the camp, to avoid hitting the Oratus.

Their targets don't ignore the sound. The warriors sitting beneath Sax burst to their feet, grouping together into parties and scrambling out into the forest. The four guards around their target shift in the noise's direction, but don't abandon their posts.

"Well trained," Sax hisses.

"They will not pose a problem," Bas replies.

And now there's a fifth one, dashing from the ranks of scrambling warriors. The quartet parts for him. One more to take care of. And quickly; the Lunare are not committing to an attack—it's a distraction and nothing more. The Oratus do not have a long window.

"We cannot wait," Sax says. He hears an agreeing hiss.

The Oratus flings himself from the tree, towards the four guards, with claws outstretched and ready.

15 / FURY FOUGHT

The second crack throws me to the ground. Not because it strikes close to me, not because it blew up the dirt at my feet or shattered the branches over my head, but because it flashes me back to the last time I fought a war, only months ago, in the deserts to the west, where bangs like these signaled my rise to Empress.

Viera's helping me up in a moment, and I notice that, in her left hand, one of her pistols is already drawn. My four Shadows spread out, forming a loose barrier between us and where the noise came from. Charre cries calling for groups to assemble, to march out in search of the enemy, ring out between the clatter of the rain.

"You're all right?" Viera says as I get to my feet.

"Fine," I say. "Just surprised. I didn't think the Lunare would attack."

"Me either."

Malo brushes through the Shadows, looking hard at Viera and I, making sure I'm not hurt.

"We're spreading out to engage," Malo says. "Though sending fire from afar isn't a normal Lunare strategy."

"They might be trying to see how we'll react, to draw us closer to their walls," Viera replies.

"My warriors know not to press that far," Malo says. "They'll stay well back of the walls, but if the Lunare can truly strike us from within their shelter, we'll need to move, Empress."

I start to agree with Malo when lightning flashes again, splitting the night apart in a wave of light. My eyes fly up to trace the bolt, and in that moment, I see a strange, unnatural shape in the leaves. I'm not the only one; the Shadows shout their alarm too. Viera pushes me behind her, drawing her other pistol. I reach for my shard, Malo pulls his kukri as the Shadows back closer to us, where they can fight as a unit.

They don't even have a chance. Bright blue bolts, things that I've never seen before, lance out like the lightning above and strike the Shadows from two sides. Four flashes, and my four guards are burning on the ground. I don't even have time to grasp what's happened before their attackers land on the forest floor in front of me.

I know immediately these are the things that Ignos fears. They match nothing except my nightmares, with their four long, clawed arms, swishing tails, and mouths full of gaping teeth. They're hissing now, too, a rasping roar that causes me to back another step.

Oratus.

"Uglier than I thought you'd be," Viera announces, then raises her pistols and fires both.

The shots strike the creature on the right, a gray-scaled menace, and it seems as though spiderwebbing cracks appear in the creatures' skin. But nothing else. No stagger, no falling to the ground or toppling backwards. Instead, the monster darts forward towards Viera, its two front claws tearing towards the Lunare's throat.

Malo jumps in front of the attack, his two kukri catching the creature's swings. The Oratus—I use Ignos' name for them automatically, like an instinct—has two more claws, though, and it uses those to grip Malo's waist and throw the warrior to the side. Viera's trying to reload, but she barely readies one before the pink-scaled Oratus is on her, using its tail to trip and then pin Viera to the ground.

Leaving me facing the two creatures alone.

"What do you want?" I ask, though I think I know.

"You are the Empress?" asks the gray-scaled one, speaking my language without issue in its rasping voice.

"I am," I say. "Why are you attacking us?"

The two Oratus glance at one another, then the pink one looks at me. "Sevora, do not try to lie to us. We know what you are."

"Sevora?" I've never heard the word in my life.

"You know what we are," the pink one continues. "I can see the knowledge in your eyes—"

"Ignos told me!" I cry, desperate to keep them from hurting Viera.

I can see Malo picking himself up from the ground, shallow cuts in his sides where the gray-scaled one had clawed him. In another moment, maybe, the warrior could take them by surprise.

"Ignos?" Now it's the gray-scaled one's turn to talk.

"My god," I say. "The voice inside my head."

"The one that came from the crashed seed?"

"Seed?"

There might be a way to survive this, Kaishi. Tell them the truth. All of it.

"It would have crashed down in the jungle. You would have found it, an oval, in a pit surrounded by rocks and burning things."

I catch Malo's eyes with my own, shake my head slightly to keep the warrior away. Based on how the gray-scaled one handled Malo's attack, I'm afraid another assault will only hurt Malo more. I'm ready to try Ignos' idea, so I begin to tell the story. I speak fast, treading lightly over details, and the two monsters listen to the entire thing.

"Mind loosening your tail?" Viera coughs. "Can't really breathe here."

I'm surprised to see the pink one listen, lift her tail slightly off the Lunare's chest. I'm not as surprised to see the grey one whip his tail suddenly, catch Malo's legs and trip him over.

"You're coming with us," the pink one says. "Now."

"Then we're going with," Viera announces.

"No," the gray-scaled one says.

"Yes," I say. "Or I'll fight you. And I don't think you want to kill me."

If they wanted me dead, after all, the two Oratus could have done that by now.

Again the Oratus look at each other, then back to me. Then the gray-scaled one takes a step forward, I see the tail twitch, and there's a sharp pain.

Nothing more.

16 / LIVING DECISIONS

They should all be dead. The three of them. One, the Empress, the young female, should be the first executed. Then the two with her in the hold, to be safe. Bas takes them for controls. To compare their natural, non-Sevora biology to the infected one.

A pointless experiment.

Sax and Bas had come to this planet to find the Sevora, and they had succeeded. One swipe of his claws and this would be dealt with. But Sax can't defy his pair so easily. Not there, in that stormy jungle. So Sax helps Bas take the three humans out. Carries them in a long sprint through the jungle, Stim packs—with Bas overcoming her distaste of the drug because of the necessity—serving to keep them moving even when exhaustion should knock them down. The scared humans don't do anything—the razor claws close to their throats a constant reminder of the consequences.

Now they're in the shuttle. The three prisoners stuffed in back. The one with the pistols, the one that had fractured Sax's mask, hadn't stopped talking. Changing between threats and questions. Sax had wanted to shut her up, suggested that one human control—the silent, wounded warrior—was enough. Again Bas refused. Said that they should try to learn as much as they could.

She somehow thinks this is a key. That the Sevora can be taken care of if the Oratus can only figure out what makes these humans so special. Sax looks from the terminal and its briefing program to Bas. He's finished sending in all the information, which is transmitting through to Evva's ship.

They'll have to wait, in orbit, to see what Evva orders next. To see what the Oratus commander wants to do with this new species. With this new problem.

"You think I'm being too soft," Bas says, reading his mind.

As always.

"We began, Bas, as an answer," Sax growls—he can't keep his frustration away. "We are the solution to the Sevora problem. And yet, here we're sparing one? We're taking a species we don't know? A species we care nothing about? Instead of completing our mission?"

"Shake the bloodlust from your eyes, Sax. Our mission is to rid the galaxy of the Sevora problem. Not kill them all."

"It's worked well so far."

"Has it?" Bas steps over to the console, switches from the briefing program to the standard data repository on every Vincere ship.

An encyclopedia of worlds, races, history. All there for reference as needed. Sax knows what she's going to pull up, watches anyway as she presses through the screens and gets to a narrative for their very own race.

A brutal history displays on the windshield, outside of which the blue-green planet spins to the left as they continue their orbit. It's a graph, mostly. A timeline covering all the major events that resulted in the two of them being here now.

"Look at all the fights. Look at all the times we meet the Sevora above one world or another. We throw everything at them for cycle after cycle. Chase them into one inevitable end after the next and then they come back." There's a heat in Bas' voice that Sax hasn't heard in a long time.

Bloodlust, the common Oratus drive to kill. It's the culmination of their passions. A mixture of instinct and love that comes together to make the Oratus into the pure devastation they ought to be. Yet in her voice now, Sax hears that same drive.

"How many times have we made it to what we said was the last seed ship. The last Sevora. Only to win and find the Sevora have already moved. That they're already growing. Then it all starts again. Billions and trillions of lives burned away. Including our own."

"Our own?" Sax looks at his claws. He still alive, so far as he can tell.

"What have we done, Sax? One trip on the Nova? One dying star? The rest is all battle. The rest is all blood and gore and claws and tearing. Risking our lives in this endless fight. Those three back there? The humans? If they hold the key to blocking Sevora control, then we must learn from them. Find out how to end this."

"What if you're wrong?" Sax replies. "What if the Sevora is lying, if it's clever, and it leaves the human to infect us? Then what? Is it worth risking everything for this?"

"I think so."

Sax rises to his full height. Bas matches him and they lock eyes.

"We are made to be weapons, Bas. We're not scientists. We don't research and design the galaxy. We're not meant to be more than swords to cleave through our enemies. We have one here." Seeing no sway in Bas' face, Sax adjusts course. "Let's compromise. If the Sevora has the creature under its control, then it's a risk. Even if it is resisting the Sevora, who's to say for how long? We can kill the infected one now. Complete the mission. Then tell Evva about the other two. They can be studied. More can be gathered from this planet."

"How long will that take, Sax? How many cycles more?" Bas isn't budging. "You don't even want to try."

"I don't want to lose us," Sax says. "I don't want something to happen that doesn't need to. We've almost won this war, Bas. Let's not lose it now by risking ourselves." He's not making a dent with her, so Sax again ups his offer. "We do this, Bas, and I'll request time. You know we've earned it. Evva will give it to us. We can go back to the Nova or somewhere else. See some of these wonders that we've been missing. And let those who know what they're doing, deal with these. The war might even be over by the time we come back."

This last overture works, though Bas accepts it with a heavy flaring from her vents and a narrow-eyed nod. She still believes, Sax knows, this is the wrong decision. But there are measures, degrees to this. Letting a Sevora break free and take over either one of them is a risk they can't take. So Bas agrees.

They'll eliminate the infected one, and keep the others for research.

The transition to the shuttle's cargo bay means squeezing through stacks of supplies. Crates and containers full of nutrient goop and Stim. In the back, using straps to keep material stable when landing, are the three prisoners. They're tied, sitting in a line with their backs to the wall.

"What do you plan to do with us now?" the talkative one says. She told Sax her name was Viera, but Sax has trouble forming the word. "Finally decide to off us? I see that mad gleam in your eye. You take us prisoner and then you kill us in cold blood."

"Not you," Sax says. He points at the infected creature, who's just coming back to consciousness. "That one."

There's no point in waiting anymore. Sax raises his right foreclaw, ignores Viera's sudden shouting. The third captive, heretofore sullen and silent, catches the mood and adds his own protests to the mix.

But there's one sound Sax cannot ignore. The sharp ding of a received transmission. Sax pauses. The noise rings throughout the shuttle, making sure it's heard throughout the ship. There's no way a response should come this fast. No way Evva should be responding. He left a long message. One that describes everything.

Yet, as with every official communication, because of the transmission time, Sax must start with the most important information.

That a new species has been found, one the Sevora do not seem to be able to control.

"Sax," Bas starts.

"Yes," Sax sighs, and he lowers his claw. "Let's see what she has to say."

The reply message is short. No doubt because Evva thinks Sax is going to do just what he's planned. Minimize the risk. Remove the hazard.

"Don't kill her. Take her to Cobalt station, at these coordinates."

The orders are succinct and clear.

A list of numbers follow. Ones easy to plug into the shuttle's navigation system. The station is a single leap away, though it's not one Sax knows. Regardless, the infected one lives.

For now.

17 / CAPTIVE VIEWS

Waking up after getting smashed in the head feels awful. A pounding pain that greets my opening eyes. I'm not exactly upset about the distraction, because what I'm looking at doesn't make any sense. It's not the stone, yellowed walls of the temples I've known. Or the green and leafy jungles I've walked my entire life. Instead it's a plurality of colors twined together with hard gray. Large cubes are stacked around me, striped labels bearing words that I can read: Nutrients. Water. I shake my head.

Jumble my brain back into place.

Ignos mashes words I don't understand. Apparently waking up just like me.

"Are you awake Kaishi?" It's Viera talking. A cool waterfall of relief cascades through me as I realize both she and Malo sit nearby. "How are you feeling? Alive?"

"I think so," I reply.

They haven't killed us yet. Why?

I don't have an answer for this question. I'm too busy staring around. Other boxes surround us in this dark space and green lights glow in globes on the ceiling. Dim. There's a thin breeze going through, though the air lacks any of the flavor I'm used to. It's plain, stale. No scent of anything. My ears catch a steady churning sound that I feel in my bones. Unnatural and constant. Things moving around me and underneath.

I fight the urge to panic, if only because Viera and Malo are looking at me with concern, and if they are stable, if they are not shrieking and yelling and crying, then I can't be either.

"Where are we?" I ask.

"I heard them call this the shuttle," Malo replies in Charre tongue, though he's learned more of mine and Viera's language in the last month, mostly, I think, because he's tired of not knowing what we're saying about him. "After they, um, knocked you out, they took Viera and I. We couldn't fight back." Malo looks away, and I can tell he's ashamed. He failed as my bodyguard.

Failed as the leader of my warriors.

"You tried," I say. "You stood up for me. You fought for me against something you had no hope to defeat."

No hope is putting it lightly.

I flash back anger against Ignos' comment. No hope to defeat them? Then why? Why weren't we prepared? Ignos had to know this was coming.

Nothing I could've done would have saved you. I was trying to move your people forward as fast as I could. We ran out of time.

This strikes me as weird. Ignos is a god. He can control time, and everything else. How could there not be enough? How could we not be prepared?

Because I'm not the only god. Because there are others who seek to fight me. And they do not wish me, or you, to succeed.

"You all right Kaishi?" Viera says again. "Is Ignos still talking? I would've thought he'd shut up about now, seeing as he's done nothing to help you."

"I'm trying to figure that out myself," I say. "He's not making sense."

"Gods seldom do."

All at once the green globes shift to red, and a low tone echoes throughout the shuttle. Words, words I am recognizing yet don't understand play out. A hissing voice calls for preparation. Says we will be leaping soon.

Leaping?

It's best if you close your eyes. It's easier that way.

As if I'm going to follow anything Ignos says now. Not after what he's done, or rather, what he didn't do.

So I keep my eyes open, and regret it.

It's as though the universe tears. Everything in front of me and around me and inside me seems to twist and shift and strain. To pull apart so far until I feel like the distance from my right hand to my left is a thousand kilometers. I'm at once everywhere and nowhere, in pain and in paradise. Then I snap back. Like a runner hitting a rock. All my senses go numb and ajar at once, so I can't feel anything except that I'm out of place.

Stay calm. It will pass.

I become aware that Malo and Viera are shouting. Tears are streaming down my face. It's a matter of retaking control of my own body. Putting myself back together again, as if I were a tree that lost all its leaves and now has to reattach them to my branches one by one.

"Stay quiet," I say to Viera and Malo. "Focus on yourselves. Find your pieces, and pull them back together."

I don't know if they understand what I'm saying, or if they even hear it, since they're still yelling incoherent nonsense. I keep talking to them anyway. Soft voices. They don't have Ignos in their heads. They have nothing telling them that it will pass, that what's happened is not fatal. But, together, the three of us bring ourselves back from the edge. Until, with Viera's face red and slack-jawed, and Malo gasping for breath, we're okay.

We're alive.

"We'll be docking shortly," the voice of the rose gold one. I recognize it, though I'm not sure where it comes from. "Congratulations. You managed to survive a leap."

Her hissing laugh echoes through the boxes.

18 / THE SPACE STATION

Cobalt hangs like a spiderweb in a dark corner of space. There's not even another star nearby. They're all twinkling in the distance. But then, that's how it is with Amigga researchers. Their projects are all so secretive—they tell the Vincere it's to avoid contamination—that they build their stations away from the habitable parts of the galaxy. Where no one knows what they're doing.

Amigga inventions appear, though, as if by magic. New ships or devices, methods for terraforming worlds or curing them from the same gone wrong. Sax knows all of his weapons, the mask, came from Amigga pursuing their own ends and passing along the benefits to the Vincere and the rest of the galaxy.

What everyone also knows, though, is that the Amigga choose what they pass on to everyone else. What they keep for themselves . . . well, Sax has no time for speculation.

Evva's orders are clear. Now that they've completed the leap, the briefing program picks up more from the commander. Sax plays it, with Bas listening nearby.

"I presume you saved the specimens. Deliver them to the station. Make sure they're taken care of. The Amigga there will handle the tests. Will look to see if there's anything we can glean from it." There's a burst there, static. When Evva's voice comes back, it's something different. Less ambient noise. She's changed locations. "Sax, Bas. I'm talking directly to you now. Avan, the captive Oratus you brought back to me from the seed ship? I've had a chance to look into what he's saying. There may be some truth to it, and some of his assertions concern the Amigga. Stay alert. If something goes wrong, save yourselves first. The specimens if you can."

And that's it. A warning with little detail.

"That's not like her," Sax says. "Something has Evva mixed up."

"Or someone's listening to her." Bas always has the more reasonable ideas. "Either way, we're here."

The station is a long, flat triangle. At the far point, there's a sphere, large and round. The station's core. Where the Amigga stays. The other two points are closer to them, and as they draw near, a white rectangle opens in the base wall. A docking bay. One large enough to accommodate several shuttles.

Which means *Cobalt* expects, or expected, some traffic, though the bay appears empty now. The initial part of docking with the station is tricky—in order to generate some gravity, *Cobalt* spins around the lone point and its sphere. Bas pilots the shuttle and has to first match_*Cobalt*'s spin velocity, then guide the shuttle closer and closer to the station. Sax watches as the white-blue glow of *Cobalt*'s inside draws near, a searing scar against the otherwise black background.

"Why are we going here?" Sax says as Bas switches the shuttle to its automated landing procedure. "If Evva thinks the Amigga might be a risk, then we should leap somewhere else. Back to the main Vincere fleet, maybe."

"She didn't say she had proof," Bas counters. "I don't think we scrub the mission on a hunch, especially with its potential."

The shuttle glides in, firing the microjets to keep from hitting the floor and ceiling—the empty bay means they aim for the open middle, so sides aren't a concern. A thick red light flares as they enter, telling

Sax that the whole bay isn't pressurized. No fancy electromagnetic shields here. Instead, the bay is clear. No loose things that might get yanked out as vacuum comes in.

A heavy airlock door, twice as tall as Sax and three times as wide, sits at the back wall, no doubt leading further into the station. The inside of the bay is all whitewashed. Not the standard Vincere military gray but gleaming pearl. Even the lights are white. Spotless, sanitized.

Sax finds it blinding.

The microjets make the landing easy, and the struts pop out beneath the craft without a problem. Behind them, the top and bottom of the massive bay door come together to seal away the cosmos. The red light begins a slow shift towards green as oxygen pumps into the room; making sure it's safe to breathe.

"It's an older station," Sax looks up from the console, where he's been digging into the encyclopedia. "Around since the start of the eighth cycle."

"So why did Evva send us here then?" Bas replies. "With what we might have, we should be at the best."

"If you were suspicious of the Amigga, if you didn't trust those in power, would you send us to the newest and the best? The Amigga getting the most attention?"

Sax surprises himself with the thought, but it fits: way out here, on this older model station, they would be far from prying eyes. The Amigga running *Cobalt* might not be part of Evva's concerns, might simply want to run its experiments out here in the dark, alone.

Except there is somebody here. Even though the bar isn't all green yet, there's motion in the docking bay. Sax catches it as it moves, and he can't categorize the thing. It's blue and globular. Resembles an Oratus, though it is very clearly not that. It has no defined features. No eyes, no mouth. Its skin is perfectly smooth, as though made from a mold. It waits near the shuttle, staring at them through the windshield.

"What is that?" Bas says.

"I don't know, but I'm going to be ready." Sax moves to put on the mask, safely stored on equipment racks in the back of the bridge—designed to ensure the Oratus piloting the shuttle are never far away from their weapons.

Even though it's damaged, the mask still serves its purpose. It wraps over his claws, his arms, his torso, and legs. Covers Sax with a seal mostly intact. Enough to provide protection, enough to hold the weapons he brings. Bas does the same with hers. When the bar outside in the bay flashes green, they give no thought to the prisoners, to the specimens.

They lower the landing ramp.

The thing moves towards them before they even reach the bottom. Holds out a gel-claw toward Sax. A traditional Oratus greeting. Both Oratus should give claws, clasp them tight. Follow with a touch of the heads to one another. A symbol of kinship, of shared purpose.

But this creature is no Oratus. Sax stares at the claw until the thing retracts it.

"Welcome, Oratus. I am Dalachite, and I see you've met my familiar," Dalachite's voice booms out through the station's intercom. It's deep and gurgling. One unused to speech. "Clever aren't they? My own invention. Looks just like you."

"This thing is an abomination," Sax says in reply. "Nothing about it is real."

He doesn't know from where the Amigga, as that's clearly Dalachite, is watching him, so Sax addresses the familiar.

"Well then, I'm afraid you'll need to overcome your prejudice. My familiars are everywhere on the station. *Cobalt* wouldn't run without them. But tell me, do you have it? The specimen?"

So Evva, or someone, has been in contact with the Amigga.

"We do," Sax says. "One of them, we believe, is infected."

"With the Sevora. Yes. It's exciting, isn't it?"

Sax almost laughs at how different his idea of exciting is from

Dalachite, but swallows the urge. Remembers Evva's private words, and asks, "What will you do with them?"

"That is not your concern, Oratus." Dalachite picks up a note of haughty irritation, as if Sax is playing at things far beyond his understanding. "You are here as my guest. You are completing a mission. I invite you to do so now. If you will give me your captives, please."

Bas goes back into the shuttle. It's an unspoken move, a tacit agreement between the two of them. Bas seems to understand the specimens more than Sax does, so she'll go bring them out. In the meantime, Sax keeps his eyes open for weapons. Any sign that this might be some sort of strange ambush. Anything that might lend credence to Evva's warning.

There's nothing. Only the blank blue of the familiar.

"How long?" Sax asked. "How long have you been on the station?"

"Since *Cobalt* was born," Dalachite replies. "You must understand, Oratus. Amigga do not travel. We do not move or take other jobs. We simply are, and we build our homes around us. *Cobalt* is as much a part of me as any organ. As my skin and bone."

That answers that. Sax can't think of anything else to say, so the two stand in silence until, with the clanking claws on metal, Bas reappears leading the three specimens behind her.

Almost at once, the blue familiar changes. The claws sink back into center mass, which shrinks down before limbs pop out again, only this time in the shape of the specimens. The tail disappears, and the legs soften. Five small flagella form on each foot, each hand.

"Delightful," Dalachite says. "It has been far too long since I had a new species to play with. Look at these. Fingers and toes? Yes. This will be fun."

"This isn't about fun," Bas speaks now. The humans are all too afraid, or struck silent by the world around them. "This is about solving the war. This is about finding a cure for the Sevora infection."

"Of course it is. Of course that's what I'll do, but first things first." The familiar, despite not being the source of Dalachite's voice, looks at the specimens. "Let's get all of you settled. Please, follow the familiar."

That's it for pleasantries. The blue thing ignores Sax completely and instead beckons the humans to follow. They stare back at it, not quite sure what it wants, until the familiar waves them forward again. Bas tells them to obey, and then the humans do. The infected woman tailed by the other two. One brown and one pale. Sax and Bas watch them go, watch the door out of the bay open and shut behind them.

"Is that it?" Bas says as they stand alone in the docking bay. "Do we leave?"

"You heard Evva," Sax is talking now through the mask, staring at Bas so the slightest whisper sends between their two masks like the clearest shout.

"So then we stay." Bas looks fine with this idea. "We stay and watch. Make sure the Amigga does as it should."

Sax agrees. He has no desire to see the humans survive. But the image of that blue, false Oratus lingers in his mind. If he finds an excuse to destroy it, he will.

19 / EVERYTHING IS NEW

Overload. That's the only way I can describe it. So many new things, so far beyond anything I'd ever thought.

They strike me one after another. First comes the shuttle. Standing up, leaving it through a strange metal ramp. Something that makes unnatural sounds as I walk upon it. My legs, my arms feel light, and with every step I feel as though I might float away. Instead, as I walk, I force my feet down. Every time I hit the ground it's a victory.

Where do I walk into? A place unlike any I've ever been before. A pure glow pours from above, and yet somehow it seems lifeless. At first I think that it must be Ignos, but then I look up, as we walk out from beneath the shuttle, and see that no, like inside the creature's ship, there are globes at in the ceiling producing these rays.

The floor is a glossy black. So shiny that I can see myself in it. The only break in the alabaster walls comes from a strange green line that seems level with the glass covering on the front of the shuttle. Malo and Viera, like me, stay quiet. There's nothing we can say that is relevant to the moment. There's nothing here that makes sense.

We're clinging to our sanity now.

This is a space station. This is what it's like to live outside your world.

Ignos is muted. The explanation is perfunctory. It's not hard to see why. I'm still angry at him. Still incensed that the god of my people can keep such things from me. That he could leave us so unprepared for what was coming. I'm starting, now, to wonder what kind of god he is. If Ignos is not all-powerful, then what is he?

I'm a guide. Your friend. The only way you'll get through this.

In that, Ignos has a point. He at least seems to know what's happening. He seems to understand, and urges me to follow when the strange blue creature waves us forward, and when the pink-gold monster seconds the command, I do.

The floor is cold on my bare feet. My skin breaks out in goosebumps as the chill air plays upon us. None of us were wearing much back in the jungle. It was the summer season. So here we are, in thin cotton capes and wraps, freezing.

We head towards the door, which is plenty tall and large for all of us. We could walk abreast if we wanted to, though something compels us to stay in single file. We're moving towards a destination, not walking for conversation, and all of us are in our own worlds.

There's magic when the door opens. In one moment, a collection of pressed silver boards stands in our way. In the next they do not. It shoots up, I think, but I'm not sure as it happens so fast. A hallway lays beyond, with branching paths and more white globes glowing in the ceiling. There's nothing on the walls except that same sterile white. I wonder if, perhaps, we died in the jungle and this is the beyond. An unknowable blankness.

You are very much alive, Kaishi. Do not forget it. Or you may not be for much longer.

The blue thing, which looks like a child's drawing of her father, leads us through. Once in the hall, its arms begin to wave, and a voice erupts out of the air. I see no mouth, I see no speaker, but sounds come through the air nonetheless. Speaking in our common tongue, and I worry that Malo will not be able to understand.

"Welcome to your new home. Welcome. It's a place where you shall find how small your old life really was. Here you will learn, here you will change. Here you will provide a great service to the rest of the galaxy." The voice gets excited with itself. Like a priest winding up towards a grand conclusion.

Only I don't like what it's saying. I've heard promises before. I've heard people both great and small talk about all kinds of wondrous things that would be coming to me. I've seen how, more often than not, those promises turn out to be lies.

The thing notices my skepticism, because the blue creature stops and turns towards me. Though it has no mouth, I hear words again, coming from everywhere.

"I see doubt in your eyes," the voice continues, and I detect wounded pride, like a hunter whose prowess I'd questioned. "Do you really think that you will be hurt here? You are prizes. You are miracles. You are my most treasured possessions."

"Possessions?" That's Viera now.

"Oh yes. You're on *Cobalt*. I am Dalachite, and you're in my home. You'll stay here as long as I need you." The blue thing spins on its heel then and continues walking.

"I don't like that word," Viera whispers as we move.

Hallways branch off of where we are. Closed doors leading I don't know where, but we go past them all. Deeper.

"I don't believe it," I say. "We might be somewhere else, but we are still ourselves. It does not own us. Doesn't have control of our bodies or our minds."

"Not yet," Dalachite says. "Up here on the right are your quarters. Each one of you has a room, and you'll ignore the rest. It may not be everything that you want at first, but we'll be working together to make it as you like. Follow my familiar and it will see to your comfort."

In turn, the blue creature leads us down a short hallway with six doors, though only three have green circles above them. At the first one, the blue man points to Malo.

"You first now. Come on." Dalachite issues the command pleasantly, as if telling us to smell a pretty flower.

"He doesn't understand you," I say. Malo's looking at me, and while I don't see fear in his eyes, I see wariness. Confusion. I translate for the creature, "It wants you to go inside."

"Should I?" Malo asks. "I'd rather stay with you."

"I don't think we have a choice. Not now."

Malo accepts the order of his Empress. He steps past me, follows the familiar's outstretched arm, and goes inside the room. The door shuts behind them as soon as he enters. We repeat the process at the next one, with Viera stepping inside, and the Lunare promises to come see me in a minute.

Now we're at the last one. My room. The door opens as the familiar approaches, and inside I see what looks like a bed. It's not a mat, it's not stuffed cloth full of cotton. It's huge, and appears to be some sort of silvery mass within a metal frame. The rest of the room is taken up by a wide black screen on one wall. On my left, across from the bed, is what appears to be a table.

"I know it seems spare," Dalachite says. "But you will be spending much time here. Sleep, as your species requires. A place to spend the occasional bit of time between sessions. You'll come to like it."

"What happens next?" I ask the familiar, because even if Dalachite's voice doesn't come from it, I need to look at something.

"Next? Next we discover who you are. How you fit together in the universe we know. Then, perhaps, some sleep. Some food."

"After that?" I say because everything Dalachite described sounds unimportant.

"Then we find out what to do with that thing inside you. The parasite that can't seem to control your mind."

And my world falls apart.

20 / A CHANGE OF PLANS

If the Oratus are going to stay on *Cobalt*, they'll have to find a way inside. They're looking at the closed door out of the docking bay. Sax wants to take his claws to it. See whether the door can handle an Oratus raking its metal. But he doesn't. This is a research station, and in the hierarchy of his galaxy, the Amigga stand apart. They are neither above nor below the Oratus but equal.

Therefore, Sax cannot go tearing up the station. Not unless he wants to pay the consequences.

"They'll kill you." Bas reads his mind, says what he's thinking. "You damage this place, the Amigga itself might do it. Or Evva, once word gets back to her."

"That's the problem," Sax says. "They put weapons in a place where weapons don't belong. How is it my fault if I do what I'm made to?"

Sax walks over to the door. Takes five long strides, each one sending tingling shivers up his legs as the claws click and resonate on the metal floor. It's a sensation that he's become use to. Living in space will do that; carpet is too expensive, too unnecessary. The door has a red light over the top. A standard make for these stations. For Vincere ships. Red means locked, green means open and blue means only for the right person. Sax guesses there's not many people on the station, so blue doesn't show up much.

"Sax." Bas' caution isn't necessary. Sax won't attack the door.

Not yet, anyway.

Instead, he raises one hand, clenches his claws together to form a fist, and is about to knock when the door swings open. It's too late though: Sax's fist is already flying forward. The blue familiar, still looking like a human, appears in precisely the wrong position.

Sax smashes the familiar's face.

It's like punching water. Sax's bony, scaled knuckles drive ripples in the familiar's face, and it blows apart. Blue ooze showers the hallway, Sax, and everything else. The mess lives, though, only for a second. The goop reverses direction, comes together, racing back towards the familiar. Rivulets returning to their owner. Sax watches a line slick its way down his leg to the floor, race over and absorb into the familiar's foot.

"Now that wasn't very nice," Dalachite says. "I don't know what they're teaching you Oratus now, but it used to be we didn't greet our partners with fists to the face."

Sax opens his mouth to make an excuse, but the Amigga tramples on.

"Not that it matters. In fact, you performed a valuable service. I've always wanted to see how my familiars would handle a strike I didn't deliver to them. And look, they're brilliant! Bio matter. I've made it myself, right here on *Cobalt.* It will always come back; electrical pulses, you see. They connect the cells, and when they're close, the energy spurs them to knit back together!"

Sax can't argue with Dalachite's results: the blue familiar is collecting itself, and already looks as though Sax didn't touch it.

"I didn't mean to," Sax grits out the apology, then moves to what he wants to say. "We're staying, at least for a little while."

"Good, good. Upon reflection, I've reconsidered my earlier position." Dalachite's enthusiasm hits Sax wrong. Why would the Amigga want them around? The answer comes a moment later, "I have many experiments that need testing, and, as you might imagine, not many find their way out to this far corner of the galaxy."

"Isn't it your choice to be here?" Bas asks, stepping up to join Sax.

"Of course, but it comes with costs. As I said, though, there'll be plenty we can do. Also, with those other specimens, it might be useful to have you around. Extra security."

As if this thing needs extra security. Sax isn't stupid. He figures Dalachite has more than one of these familiars. Those hands, watery though they are, look like they could hold a weapon if they had to. Maybe this is what Evva was talking about, maybe this is what she meant when she said to stay ready.

The familiar leads them down the hallway, and they take a swift right instead of going straight. They walk through a wide room, with several tables. Clearly a dining hall, and meant to hold far more than the zero occupants it has now. Bas asks the obvious question, "Where is everyone?"

"Like I said, *Cobalt* is an old station. The research I perform doesn't require much in the way of extra crew, so why pay for all the nutrients? Why pay for the extra facilities? We disembarked the last batch of scientists a cycle ago. As you can probably tell, it's been lonely. I'm happy to have you here."

Sax is unimpressed with what he can see of the food stores. The same sort of nutrient goop they have on the shuttle, and it's not even the flavored kind. This *is* an old station. He starts to tell Bas that maybe they shouldn't stay here all that long or they might go crazy, but then notices the familiar is staring right at him. Even without eyes, Sax can feel the thing's attention, and it makes his tail twitch.

"The experiments, friends. There are things I've been trying to train with my familiars. You see, they are my first and last line of defense. They are also my greatest project. Yet, sparring against myself is somewhat limiting. Would you mind?"

"Would we mind what?" Sax asks.

"Training my familiars? The design, I mean. A little bit of exercise will teach them quite a lot. Think of it as a way of paying me back for using my station. For eating my food."

"It's a leap to call this food."

"And it's a leap to say you're pleasurable company," Dalachite replies. "We're both making compromises here. So let's do the best we can, shall we?"

Sax glances at Bas, and his pair shrugs. "Both of us?"

"Oh no, just one of you. For now. This familiar will guide the other to your quarters."

"I'll unload the shuttle if you want to take the first round," Bas says.

Sax knows that means Bas is going to go and get herself armed. Get ready to blaze to the rescue if Sax needs it. It's an easy ask to accept.

Then the familiar is guiding him back out of the mess and into a deep maze of hallways. The first thing Sax is going to do when he gets a moment is pull up the map to this place and memorize how to get from here to there. He doesn't like being lost. It makes it all too easy to fall into a trap.

Or an ambush.

The familiar leads Sax into a large room. Cavernous, even. Unlike the other rooms, light green padding covers the floor and walls.

There's a cabinet in one corner, and its shaded red. The standard color for aid. This isn't just a sparring room for familiars, this is a training area for many things. The blue familiar walks to the center of the room and then shivers. Its hand and feet grow and droop. Its chest and shoulders shrink.

The familiar's limbs pool on the ground, split apart, and then build up again into another person. In seconds, there are two familiars standing in front of Sax, each one slightly smaller, shorter, and thinner than the first.

"Aren't they wonderful?" Dalachite says. "Of course, I'm going to have them use this new form. An Oratus takes up too much mass. They would be quite small."

"What do you want me to do?" Sax says. "If I even touch them, they break to pieces."

"To start with, how about we get an idea of their speed. Try and track them."

There's a lilt to Dalachite's voice that tells Sax it has full faith in its creations. That the Oratus will fail, and fail badly.

The Amigga is wrong.

The two familiars jump back from Sax, going in opposite directions and running towards the walls. Sax watches for a moment, gets the lay of their lines, and makes tracks for the closer one, heading toward the wall to his left. It's strange chasing something that has no defined body, that appears to be liquid moving in a mold. But then, Sax has encountered many strange creatures in his life.

Every one had a weakness.

When the familiar reaches the wall, a breath ahead of Sax, it doesn't stop. It doesn't press back, or turn and cower at the oncoming Oratus. No, it starts running up the surface. Its feet suction to the sides and the familiar heads directly above Sax. The problem is, Sax can jump. Far. He presses his legs and leaps, four claws outstretched, straight towards the familiar's back as it climbs the wall. Sax is ready to grip, to sink those claws in and start to tear.

But there's nothing to grip onto. Sax simply passes right through the familiar and explodes it into a raining shower of blue gel. The familiar's pieces splatter down to the room's floor while Sax manages to catch the wall with his talons and digs his claws into the soft surface.

The Oratus twists his head around. Stares at the puddles beneath him as they gather and form again.

"Not fast enough." Dalachite sighs. "Something to improve for future iterations. Still, let's keep going."

"Keep going with what?" Sax says, hanging from the wall.

"Based on the speed of your movements, it's unlikely my familiars will be able to dodge or outrun you. So let's change the game. Why don't we try a little bit of combat. Put you on the defensive for a change."

"Oratus don't go on the defensive."

"If you say so."

Beneath Sax, the familiar he'd exploded reforms into its human-like shape. As Sax watches, both of the familiars go over to the red cabinet and open it. Inside, Sax can see the shelves that had once been used to hold aid kits, bandages, or emergency medical supplies.

Now, though, the cabinet is full of danger; miners, and weapons of a more personal nature.

Each of the familiars pick out sharp blades, nearly a meter long. Ones that curve upwards, towards the wielder, the closer they come to the tip. The familiars turn back to Sax, set themselves apart, and wait.

Giving Sax one chance to look at his options.

Then they rush forward, their steps synchronized, and hit the floor at the same time. Sax is on the wall, which is good, as he's out of the reach of those swords. Until he remembers that they can climb. The two familiars reach the side beneath Sax and, again, start running up the wall towards him. Both of them raise the swords high over their heads to deliver what looks like a strong overhead smash.

It's almost like they don't realize the Oratus has a tail. Before they hit striking range, Sax twists and sweeps his tail across the wall, slicing through their fragile bodies. At the sudden loss of cohesion, the whole watery mess tumbles down to the floor.

One of the swords lands point first, sticking up like a monument to the defeat.

Dalachite doesn't say anything this time. It doesn't have to: the familiars show that the fight isn't over. The blue liquid pulls together, now as one, and rises into a full Oratus shape. Four arms, two legs and the tail, though the end result is smaller than Sax. The familiar picks up the blades, one in each of its two foreclaws. This time, it keeps its distance.

"So it's a coward now," Sax says to the room, hoping the Amigga can hear.

"It's learning," Dalachite replies. "Every time you defeat it, my familiar will adapt."

It'll have to adapt a lot before it poses a threat to Sax. He detects a slight twinge in his stomach. The fight is so boring that Sax is getting hungry. Time to finish this. "You want me to attack?"

"I want you to treat it as an enemy," Dalachite says. "Because, be assured, that's how it's treating you."

Fine.

Sax digs his legs into the wall. If the Amigga wants to see how Sax treats his enemies, it's in for a show.

21 / THE TRUTH

Taken as a whole, revelations haven't spiked my life regularly, which is why I'm still reeling from the last few months. I've been torn away from my family, shoved into the highest points of a rival civilization, and then stolen away by things spawned from the darkest nightmares in less time than two seasons. Through it all, I'd had Ignos. Either directly in my mind, or, before that, as a source of strength when nothing else worked.

Kaishi?

Is it all a lie? My father's belief? My tribes' faith that the world we live in is presided over by a just, if uncompromising force?

You need to calm down. Think. Listen to me.

The sacrifices. So many people. So many hearts torn out on the stone slabs. All of it for nothing. I can't—

STOP!

I blink. My world shifts back from hazy tears. They blur the blank walls, and the otherness of my gray-white prison threatens to jar me back into despair.

It's true, Kaishi. I'm not your god.

Perhaps it's the frankness of the admission, or maybe, like a boulder on the edge of a slope, I'm about to lose control anyway, but the words bend my confusion towards anger. I have a target.

So I fire.

It's not words I send after the thing in my mind but indistinct heat, torching rage and betrayal. Shot after shot of broken trust and shattered spirit. If this thing had been standing in front of me, I would be screaming. As it is, I clench my hands so tight that I feel my nails biting into my own skin. I don't let up.

Ignos—I know, now, that's not its name but I can't think of another at this blind-fire moment—recoils. Whether I'm actually causing it pain, I don't know. I don't care. It needs to know what it's done. How it's ruined everything.

Have I, though?

Of course it has! Look at where we are? What we're doing?

You saved your people, didn't you? Your tribe?

Yes, that might be true. But the way—

Your work forged an alliance between your own people and the Charre, did it not? And the miracles I gave you? Won't that ensure their strength for seasons to come?

Ignos hammers me with logic, and I struggle to keep up my raging. At home, in the jungle and surrounded by friends and family, I would have brushed aside those arguments, would have pushed and fought and scrabbled until my point was made. Here, though, where I'm on unstable ground, Ignos' words stabilize. Present the possibility, the proof that, perhaps, I'm not a complete failure for trusting some strange creature from beyond the sky.

I realize my panic, my tears and anger are not because of my people, my family or the Solare.

It's all about me.

A knock on the door comes through muffled, light, lifeless. Without the chords of real wood. Still, I look towards it and the act helps keep the clouds at bay.

"You can come in," I call.

There's a moment's hesitation, then a reply comes through, "I don't think I can, actually."

It's Malo and I'm up in an instant. The door sits in its frame; a raised pearl band looping around an entry twice my height. Compared to the openings in our family home and even the great Charre buildings, it's massive. There's no handle. I try pushing on it, but the door doesn't react.

"Do you know how to open it?" I look around the door as I ask the question.

There's a black nub to the right of the doorway; a protruding half-sphere that seems to stare at me. I touch it with the tip of my finger and it's hard. Cool and smooth, too smooth for natural rock.

"When I approached my door, it just opened," Malo replies. "Can you see anything?"

It's me.

I pause.

The door. It's detecting my presence and is locking you inside.

Makes sense. Why wouldn't Ignos continue wrecking my life?

There is a way past it, of course.

I wait for a list of requirements. Some elaborate ceremony I must perform to placate the black nub.

No ceremony. Ask. Ask the Amigga that runs this station to open the door.

I don't know what an Amigga is, so I assume Ignos is talking about the blue creature.

Dalachite, Kaishi. The voice that's always listening here. Ask it.

So I do.

"Dalachite, I don't know what you are," I say to the air, and as I speak, I hear Malo ask what I'm doing and ignore him. "But can you open my door? I don't know how."

"I can open the door for you," Dalachite says. "But, were I to do so, I would need your assurance, your promise that you would not attempt to leave."

"Leave?" I reply.

"Your chamber. You must stay inside unless my familiars come to take you."

"What? Why?"

"Oh, it's very simple, really. You see, I have much to learn about you. There are two ways I can do that: either I take you, leaving you intact, and we learn together—that's what I would prefer—however, if that becomes too dangerous, if there's a chance the Sevora inside your head could leave or infect another, then it's safer to paralyze you. Extract those components of your nervous system that allow you to move. Then, I will learn what I can."

I recall the blue familiar. It hadn't held a weapon, hadn't seemed threatening. Yet, the ease with which Dalachite speaks of hurting me . . .

It can do all it says and worse. Listen to it, Kaishi. Our chance will come later.

"I won't leave," I say to the voice.

A second later the door shoots open, and Malo steps inside. Without waiting, he wraps me in a hug, and I return the gesture. It's nice, feeling those arms around me. Nice feeling some support of any kind, really. Even though, beneath Malo's wiry muscles, there's tension.

The same fear tightening my bones.

"Where are we?" Malo whispers the words, but they're a question I can't answer.

"Far from home," I give the only reply I can. For now, it's enough.

"Home," Malo squeezes hard, then releases and steps back. "Do you think we'll see it again?"

"I think you might," I say. "Dalachite keeps talking to me like I'm some sort of experiment. Something that's been discovered. I don't think it's going to let me go."

We will make them.

"I won't leave you," Malo says. "You're my Empress."

I laugh. I can't help it. "Malo, I'm a lie. A fraud. This thing, this thing in my mind? It's not Ignos. It's just another creature. It used us."

I can tell by the way Malo's face screws up that he doesn't understand.

"You see that blue thing out there? The one that led us here? And the two monsters that took us from the jungle? It's like them," I'm shouting now but I don't realize it. "It's from somewhere else. It's inside me and it's talking to me and it's pretending. It wants us to do things for it, Malo. It doesn't care about our people. Just itself."

Mutually beneficial, Kaishi. What helps me helps you. Do you see that?

I ignore Ignos. It's not hard now. Before, pushing it away felt like I was rejecting my own god. The core of my childhood and my tribe. Now, now it's like batting away an annoying fly. I do it without a second thought.

"It doesn't matter," Malo settles his face into a straightforward stare. "You're still you. I'm still me. We'll think of some way to get out of this."

"You're still you," I say. "But I'm about as far from me as I've ever been. I left my family. My people. All for this thing in my head."

"But you still have friends. You have me."

I hear a shunt from the hallway, and before I can deliver another surly, annoyed crack to Malo, Viera appears. Her eyes crisscross between Malo and I, and then her mouth curls into a sardonic smile.

"I see it let Malo out first," Viera says in Lunare.

"Talk so Malo can understand," I reply to Viera.

"Only saying that it's nice to see you two," Viera replies in Charre.

Suddenly there's tension in the room. I don't know why Malo only replies to Viera's words with a curt nod. It seems like we should all be sticking together. That we're so far from what we know, that the three of us are all any of us has left. So I try to cut it.

"I'm sorry," I say to Malo. "I'm torn right now. But you're right.

We have to help each other. If we want to go home, we'll have to work together to find a way."

Be careful what you say. Or rather, how you say it.

I make the connection: Dalachite, the voice that comes out through the walls, it talks in the same tongue Viera and I use. But the Charre, Malo, their language is different. The voice might not understand it, might not know what passes between our lips. I warn the other two to stick to speaking Charre, and there's no argument.

"We know one way off of the station," Viera says. "That's the way we got here."

"I remember how to get back to it," Malo says. "If we can get there, perhaps we can figure out how their . . . thing works."

We fumble for the words. For a way to describe the ship. I realize I'm still wearing the answer. I looked down to my bracelet, the Cache. It's still on my wrist.

"I have this," I say and nod at the artifact. "It can help us, but I need time. Time to learn how to use it, to understand this station."

"Then we'll give you time," Malo says. "However much you need. I will defend you."

"Defend? I'll be happy if we just don't die." Viera looks back down the hallway. "Speaking of dying, one of those blue things is on its way back. Guessing this meeting is about over."

Viera isn't wrong. A few seconds later, the Lunare steps inside the room to make way for another blue familiar. It doesn't even look at either my friends, but points at me with a smooth aqua finger.

"Time for your first session, specimen. Please, follow the familiar," Dalachite says over the speakers.

I feel my friend's nervous stares, but they can't do anything for me here. Dalachite said it prefers me alive, so I have to trust that I'll stay that way.

At least for a little while.

22 / SAMPLE TEST

A long leap carries Sax over the familiar's head. Above the swords that could swing and catch him mid-flight. Sax rolls as he hits the ground, using his tail to push him along the somersault to the far end. Near where the red cabinet sits ajar, gleaming with weaponry.

He hears the familiar's feet along the ground, though it's a sad, soft pounding. Not true Oratus claws. Sax could use his, but those swords have reach. Instead he darts for the cabinet.

Sax reaches in and grabs a pair of short miners, spins around as the familiar closes, and pulls the trigger. The familiar should blow to pieces. Energy should glance out and pierce that silky smooth blue skin and burst it into puddles. But when Sax pulls the triggers, nothing happens. There's a quick click, but the deadly rays don't come. The familiar continues moving forward, sweeping those swords up and sending them crashing towards Sax.

So Sax does what he can and throws the miners up to block. The swords strike with a loud shrieking noise as they cut into the metal weapons. They don't get all the way through; the blades catch on the bottom half of the barrels. Sax feels the jerk and gets an idea.

With his foreclaws, Sax throws the miners to the left. The

swords, caught within, yank out of the familiar's grasp and fly along with them. They hit the wall, but Sax isn't seeing that. He's already moving forward, his mid-claws taking swipes at the familiar.

The weakness of Dalachite's creation is made plain. It tries to intercept Sax's attack. Tries to catch Sax's claws with its own. But there's no strength there. No solidity. Every one of Sax's claws runs straight through the familiar and tears apart its arms. Rends its legs. Until the Oratus, or what was supposed to be one, is yet again a splatter on the floor.

"Do you know what your issue is, Amigga?" Sax calls to the voice, blue slime dripping from his mouth after an eager bite. "Your familiars don't have weight. Enough reality. You want to fight something like me, then you need to give your familiars bodies that work."

There's nothing for a while. The familiar cells flow together into a pool and stay there. Sax, bored at the silence, goes over to where the miners and swords sit and picks them up off the ground, separates them. Takes a closer look.

The miners are standard issue, if, like so many other things on the station, somewhat out of date. They lack the power of Sax's own weapons; unable to punch through heavy walls, like the seed ship gateways. The swords, meanwhile, are nothing better than training weapons.

They're missing the capability of the ones Sax has used before. A slot in the hilt to allow the blades to retract and extend. Wiring for heating in case the blade has to cut through metal. A feature that would have, should have let the weapons carve through Sax's improvised defense.

Minutes pass and Sax goes to the door, but it's not open. He can't find any way to make it so. He tries calling out to Dalachite, but receives no response. For a moment Sax wonders if he's going to die in there. Starve out, or suffocate as punishment for the insult he's delivered to the Amigga's creations.

"I'm sorry," Dalachite announces with no warning. "I had to deal with another matter. I see you've made short work of my experiment."

"Short work is an understatement."

"Yes. But my familiars are new. You have had cycles to develop and refine. I will not be discouraged. Neither is it fair to expect an Oratus to fight like a robot, or punish you for your success. I'll unlock the door, and you may proceed."

"I'm doing this to be nice, Amigga," Sax says. "I'm not your prisoner, or your plaything. Next time, let me come and go as I please."

"Of course, Oratus. Of course."

The door shunts open and Sax leaves the training room. Heads back down the hallways, this time using his vents to guide him. Smelling the scent of cooking food. Of nutrient goop heated up into its edible state. The smell of Bas; a sweet, strong scent that says his pair has been busy too.

When he comes to the kitchen this time, Bas has an array of colored bars spread out on the table. Nutrient goop starts out as such: a soft spongy liquid, but when heated hardens into a cracker. One packed full of vitamins and energy. Stimulants and steroids to keep muscles strong in space, where such things, with little gravitational resistance, fall into rapid decline.

"I've unloaded what we need," Bas says as Sax enters. "Found our quarters."

"I won." Sax waits for Bas to congratulate him, but his pair only laughs, a short hissing sound.

"Are you expecting an award? I'd have been more insulted had you lost to something that Amigga made."

Sax would agree, but the fight is sticking with him. How quickly the familiar changed and adjusted holds a headache in Sax's mind. So he tells the narrative to Bas. Explains the back and forth. Describes how the familiar could split, and how it could use the weapons.

"The miners weren't charged this time," Sax finishes. "But they could've been. They will be one of these times. I have no doubt. Dalachite is going to try to kill us."

"If that's as you say, then we're outnumbered," Bas replies. "You and I can kill an army, but not one that keeps coming back."

"Unless we eliminate the source," Sax replies.

"Not yet," Bas says. "Not yet, Sax. We can either kill Dalachite now, and render this whole trip worthless, the specimens unexamined and our potential solution to the Sevora problem unexplored. All for a hunch. All because you're afraid. Or, we prepare."

Prepare. This makes more sense. Hope for the best, be ready for the worst. Common wisdom.

Sax has an idea for that.

"Did you happen to find where the humans are?"

"Yes." Bas nods to a side of the kitchen, where a console sits in the wall, its black screen displaying nothing. "The blueprints for the station are on there. Maps. I think I know where they are."

"Then after this, I'll see to our preparations." Sax sits down at the table, wraps his tail around his waist, and begins to bite into the flavorless, crunchy, bars.

They're better than the blue familiar ooze, but not by much.

23 / SESSIONS

The room is spherical, with a small platform extending out from the door into the middle. There's nothing there, on the platform, except for the shiny pearl metal that covers everything on Cobalt. The familiar directs me out to it anyway. The voice hasn't talked much on the way here, as if it's become distracted by something.

I make the walk to the platform in silence.

Ignos, though, keeps talking.

This is an immersion chamber. They'll test—

Stop it. Be quiet. I'm still reeling from learning what Ignos really is, and every time the creature buzzes my mind, I start to panic. Worry that Ignos is going to manipulate me again. Tell me something I want to hear that helps its own ends.

On the platform I can look around me. It's not an exceptionally high sphere, though I think it's tall enough for one of the Oratus to stand where I do. Certainly more than twice my own height above and below. The paneling, though, catches my eye: interlocking rectangles, and the lines between each of them pulsate in different colors. Waves of yellow and orange and blue and green cascade around the sphere. It's mesmerizing, unnaturally beautiful.

I hear the door shut.

I'm trapped in this room, and for the first time since getting on the station, I feel hungry. Biological needs. But all of that quickly goes away when the lights go out and plunge me into darkness.

"This is meant to give me an idea of who you are. How your mind and body operate," Dalachite says these things with a falling edge, as if it's reading a script while doing something else.

I don't have a chance to ask what that is, because novas appear in front of my eyes. A series of wild flashes and I'm about to stumble back, when I realize the platform I'm on has changed. My feet were on smooth metal, they're now locked. Bands have come over them, sealing me down. It's uncomfortable, and I feel like I could break my legs if I try hard enough, but the bands keep me stable while the world explodes around me.

That's the only way I can describe it. Bright lights burst one after the next in myriad colors. After a few seconds of this I shut my eyes, squeeze them tight and try to make it go away. Even behind my eyelids I can see the splashes until they stop and darkness returns.

When I open my eyes, I see nothing, but now I feel a breeze. Wind picking up, though I'm not sure where it's blowing from. The air whirls around the chamber and it gets very cold. So cold that I shiver and my teeth chatter against each other.

"Stop," I try to say, and my words gasp out as steamy breath in front of me.

As if Dalachite is listening, the wind slows to a crawl, then stops entirely before starting back up in the opposite direction. This time, hot. So hot. I begin to sweat as it feels like I'm standing in the desert, underneath the burning heat of Ignos.

It's still black.

Before I can breathe, before I can say anything, the air stops and the room equalizes its temperature. Back to the same cool nothing as everywhere else on the station. A small circle appears in front of me. A light. It begins to move. I follow it around with my eyes, as there's not much else I can do standing there on the platform. I wonder at the point of all this is, but I'm trapped and I'm scared and I don't know what else to do, so I watch.

The circle goes too far left, to the point where I cannot follow. My head turns and then I twist my body to track it until I can't rotate anymore without snapping my hips apart. The dot hovers at the edge of my vision, then swings back and does the same in the opposite direction. Then it centers directly in front of me. Grows brighter, so bright that again I squint and then it dims suddenly and disappears.

In the dark in front of me images appear. Things I don't recognize. Strange vistas, orange and green. Churning oceans with white ice formations arcing across in the background. More and more flash in front of me, staying only for a second or two.

Until one. One that makes me gasp. One that makes tears come to my eyes. It's a grove of trees, with vines hanging from their branches, sloping towards a fern-covered ground. In the back, almost hidden, I can make out a small river flowing by. I've not seen the exact place, but it feels to me of home. It is so much home.

The picture fades away to nothing.

I hear clanking and grinding machines, a word I've come to know from Ignos' inventions. I feel things running along my body. Cold, metal. Poking at my skin and I try to reach to brush them off, but as I do so something grabs my arm. More bands. In the dark I cannot see, but they feel to me as if they're coming from the same place, the same platform that is still holding my feet.

Pain. Brutal sharp and brief. It travels from my arm down my body to my legs and back up again. As if testing each and every part of me.

"Very good, Kaishi," Dalachite says as the pain fades. "You are a fascinating specimen. Something I never expected to see. I have one final test for you. One last thing. So if you would please, relax."

"I," but that's all I can manage. My body is exhausted, my mind burns after what's just happened, and all I can do is slump into the metal holding my arms and legs.

The door opens, and footsteps come towards the platform. I turn my head to look, but as I do so the door shuts again and anything coming close is shrouded in dark. A moment later I feel chill fingertips touching my head. Only these are not the fingertips I know. These don't have the rich texture of human hands.

These don't have the warmth of a human's body. No, these are lifeless and slick, like being grabbed by a drop of water. They hold my head straight. I feel something long begin to sneak into my ear. It keeps going and going and going and fear pours out of Ignos, so much that I'm nauseated by it.

A twitch and a vibration and I'm aware, for the first time, of what Ignos *is*. There's a frenzy in my mind. In my head. As though thousands of skittering feet are running between my ears scratching and grabbing everything they can. The sensation is followed by a throbbing aching blast that would have me on my knees if I were capable of falling.

Then it's over. The object withdraws, foot steps recede. The door opens and shuts again.

The chamber lights come on slow, and once the whole room is cast in that same alabaster white as the rest of the station, the restraints pull away.

I fall on my knees, plant my hands on the cool metal and cry.

24 / TRAINING ALLIES

Sax leads the humans, who call themselves Viera and Malo, through the last hallway to the training room. It wasn't hard getting Dalachite's permission for the exercise, as the researcher wants to learn about the specimens as much as Sax wants to train them.

"So what are you?" Viera asks as they walk. "I understand you came from the sky. From wherever this place is."

"I did not come from here," Sax replies. "I live, if you wish to call it that, far away. On a ship much larger than this station."

"Station, ship . . . I'm thinking these mean different things to you than they do to me. I'm guessing you don't paddle your way around?"

"Paddle?"

Malo, the other one, mutters something Sax can't understand.

"I'm not joking." Viera says. "It's a question. Rather than sit silent like you, I'm trying to figure out what's going on here."

Sax glances from one to the other. The humans exhibit courage in the face of danger and unknown circumstances. A healthy sign. Sax gives them a quick lesson on space travel, on how leaping creates folds in the universe to take a ship from one end to the other, and by the gradual glazing of their eyes, knows when he's said enough.

"Another thing," Viera says as soon as Sax falls silent. "The other one, with pink scales? She comes from the same place as you? Is she your sister?"

"We are called Oratus," Sax says. "The 'pink one' is my pair. My mate for life."

"Yeah, we humans try to do that too." Viera shrugs. "Always seemed too much trouble to be worth it."

Sax stops. Presses the tip of his tail against Viera's chest and turns to look at her. "I don't care about your society or your species, except as it can help us stop the Sevora from infesting the galaxy."

"So would you say Bas is the nice one?"

This is wasting too much time. Sax doesn't answer, but lopes on.

When they reach the training room door, the light above already shines green; Dalachite following through on its promise. Sax leads the way in and gestures with a single foreclaw towards the center.

"Stand there till I say otherwise," Sax orders with a sharp hiss, and then he heads towards the cabinet.

Inside, much the way he left them, are the two damaged miners, a collection of smaller arms, and the swords.

Where to begin.

With a visceral lesson, obviously.

Sax grabs two small miners and turns back to the humans.

"Watch," Sax says and raises the miners, aims one at each of the two humans, and pulls the triggers.

Azure bolts flash out for a split second and strike each of the humans. They both twitch, then fall. Collapse without a sound onto the floor. Sax laughs, then walks over and stares down at the pair.

"Do you see?" Sax hisses. "These are stunning miners. Packed full of energy, they will overload your nervous system and fry your mind for a short period. Useful, because stunning shots use a relatively small amount of power. Which means you can fire over and over again."

To demonstrate, Sax points the weapons at the humans and, just as Viera and Malo start to move their eyes towards the Oratus, Sax shoots them a second time. "These will not slow down a large creature at all. They will not keep anyone, even at your small size, paralyzed for long. So it's best to use these in an emergency. To buy yourself time, or to surprise someone expecting something different."

Sax replaces the stunning miners in the cabinet and pulls out one of the heftier weapons. One not broken. He strides back to the middle the room. Viera and Malo are blinking now, coughing. Trying to find their nerves.

"This a full miner. It can fire like so," Sax pulls the trigger and bright red flashes out and digs into the side of the room.

The laser light burns into the padded walls, leaving the metal beneath clean.

"Quick, lower powered shots still capable of doing plenty of damage to the right target. Or, if you don't mind burning through your power, you can use it like this."

Sax adjusts where he places his claws, causing a different set of small colored circles on the side of the miner to illuminate a deep red, and he pulls the trigger. This time, instead of a single flash, a steady stream of molten energy shoots forth. The frothing red beam torches the padding, disintegrating it as the beam moves. Sax keeps blasting for a few seconds, careful to shift his aim so as not to actually burn through the room's wall to the other side.

"Now that's a weapon," Viera says from the floor.

Or rather, tries to. Sax catches the words, interprets the meaning, but the sound is more a squeaking rasp than anything. Her vocal cords still not working the way they should.

"Both of these will help you should you need to fight," Sax says. "Later, you'll have the chance to fire all of these. Learn how not to blow yourself to tiny, tasteless ash."

Sax goes and gets the swords. By the time he gets back to the center of the room, both Malo and Viera are standing again, though neither looks particularly thrilled.

"They don't stun too, do they?" Viera nods at the swords as Sax walks up.

"They don't have to," Sax replies. "Why stun when you can kill?"

Malo says something to Viera again, and the human shrugs.

"Do you not speak our language?" Sax asks.

"Little," Malo replies.

"The man has his own tongue. He understands most of what we're saying, just not how to talk back," Viera explains. "I'll translate."

Malo repeats what he said a moment ago. Viera replies with a curt line, then turns to Sax.

"Malo says that killing is wasteful." Viera shrugs. "Can't sacrifice a dead human."

"Sacrifice?"

"Right. You win a fight, you take the prisoner, then carry them to the top of some temple or somewhere, take out their heart and ask your gods for stuff." Viera talks as though she's describing the dullest dirt in the galaxy. "You monsters do something similar?"

"We eat our prisoners."

True enough for these humans, anyway.

Viera laughs, tells Malo, who proceeds to look ill, which only makes Viera laugh harder.

"See, Malo has a deep love for his people," Viera continues to Sax. "He has this idea that they're the chosen ones. That they're going to wind up ruling our planet. And, I suppose, this galaxy you keep talking about."

Now it's Sax's turn to laugh. Viera points at the Oratus, then says another series of words to Malo. The human warrior, for Sax can tell Malo's profession in that way a fighter can see himself in another, doesn't appreciate whatever Viera says. He pushes away his friend and holds out a hand to Sax.

"Think he wants the sword," Viera says.

"That much is clear." Sax gives Malo the blade. The warrior

turns and points the tip of it at Viera. "I believe you have insulted him."

"Believe I did," Viera replies, shaking her head. "We would have wiped his civilization away if Kaishi hadn't found a creature with all the answers in her head. Guessing Malo is still feeling sore about that."

A rivalry, with a deeper anger to it. These emotions are dangerous. Not something Sax wants to contend with if, or when, he needs these two fighting alongside him and Bas. Best to purge such feelings early. He holds the second sword out to Viera, who takes it and spins the hilt in her hand.

"You'll find gravity is lower here than on your home world," Sax says. "Your moves won't have quite the same speed. Swing light and learn from each other."

Sax steps back until his tail touches the room's wall and waits. Viera looks at her sword, then over at Sax. "What are you wanting us to do? Whack away?"

Sax nods.

Malo says something then, and Viera sighs back at the warrior. Spreads her feet and sets the sword in the middle, with both hands on the hilt. Malo bends his knees slightly, leans forward and holds the sword at a flat angle. There's time for a single breath. Viera makes the first move. Steps into a sweeping cut at Malo. But the gravity is low, and the momentum from her lunge is too much to stop.

Viera floats as she tries to swing, tumbling forward. Malo, looking to take advantage, swipes up his sword for an overhead cut, but that motion too brings Malo up off the floor just a bit. Enough to throw him off balance and together the two of them fall gently to the ground in a crumpled heap.

Sax can't help it, he laughs; loud hisses ringing through the chamber.

The two fighters untangle themselves, once again taking up their positions. Viera lets words fly, and Sax catches the name, Kaishi, of the third human. Interesting. Perhaps she is the real center of this conflict.

Malo relaxes his guard, opens his mouth to unleash some retort, when Viera charges. She doesn't even lead with the sword, instead she bends her right leg and shoves off, throwing her left foot into a kick that catches Malo's face. The warrior flies back, bounces into the wall. The gravity gives Malo enough time to catch himself, plant his hand on the ground and kneel, looking up towards Viera, who's laughing.

"This gravity thing. It's great," Viera says to Sax as she hops, goes a meter in the air and sinks back down.

Malo yells something full of heat, and then he's on his feet rushing forward. Viera touches on the ground just as Malo arrives, the charging warrior swinging his sword in a crossing slash, with enough control not to send himself spinning. Viera manages to block the swing, angling Malo's weapon down to the floor. Viera follows the guard with a left-hand slap, again to Malo's face, and the warrior staggers back.

"Don't get angry now, Charre," Viera says. "There's a reason the Lunare were winning before Kaishi intervened. You're outdated. You're all pathetic."

Sax can see something though. It's in Malo's eyes. In his bearing as the warrior stands back up. Viera continues to fling insults, though Sax thinks Malo isn't hearing them anymore. He's in the fight, as any true warrior should be, and this kind of fight ends only one way.

Sax needs to stop this now. This isn't a training exercise anymore.

"I mean think about it. Your army spends all this time working with sacrifices. Slaughtering defenseless people on top of Tiers or your giant temples? How is that helping you?" Viera gestures with the sword. "Know what? It's not. Not at all. I wouldn't be surprised, by the time we get back, to find we have all of you in chains working our mines."

When Malo attacks again, he gives no signal. Only a slight tightening of his arms. Then Malo launches himself. Pushes both feet into the ground and dives forward with his blade pointed straight at Viera like a missile. A move impossible in higher gravity. One Sax suspects Viera has no training for. No preparation. No idea how to defend. She swings the sword, tries to block, but Viera is too slow.

Malo strikes, dives the point deep into Viera's chest.

And Sax fears he's killed a human.

25 / ORDINARY EXTRAORDINARY

I step through the halls. A familiar guides me. Its blue hands reach out and hold mine, pulling me along as I try to fix myself. I'm reaching through the stories of my childhood, the ones about our god Ignos, about humans and animals and survival and triumph that provide examples of how to deal with this sort of trauma.

I find nothing.

There's no Solare story for this. No legend or tale told around the fire that says what to do when you find out how easy you are to break. I was poked and prodded on that platform. Tested and torn. My body made to dance for some unknown reason, for some creature I don't know or understand.

Which brings me to a question. Which gives me a way forward.

"What was that?" I ask the familiar—my first words since I left the platform.

"I'm getting to know you," Dalachite replies from the walls around me. The familiar keeps us walking. "The start of a long and fruitful relationship for both of us."

Fruitful.

Long.

I'm not sure I'll last through more of those.

As if it's reading my thoughts, Dalachite continues, "These first conversations might be difficult. Painful, even. But that's natural. What discoveries happen without such hardship? Where would we be without the willingness to endure strife to gain what we need?"

"I don't see you enduring anything."

Careful, Kaishi. This one has the power to kill us at any moment it chooses.

Which might be a relief. In any case, I've said the words, so, while we walk, I wait for the voice to respond.

"I'll forgive you that one, specimen." Dalachite chooses not to use my name. "What I've endured is beyond your comprehension. What I have lived through, sacrificed for the good of the galaxy, is so far beyond your short trial that it doesn't bear mentioning. Go now, recover, and know that you have much more to give before you can claim yourself a martyr."

I don't want to be a martyr. I don't care about the galaxy—something I didn't know existed until hours ago. I just want to go home.

Then fight your way back.

I will.

We're not heading back to my room. I only notice—as most of the hallways look the same—because we've been walking longer than it took to get to that terrible platform.

"Where are we going?" I ask, but the familiar doesn't stop and Dalachite doesn't respond.

Eventually we reach another door and the familiar opens it with a blue palm on a black box to the door's right. A whoosh and its open. I freeze. A creature stands on the other side. The pink and gold one. Outside of the jungle, of the panic that consumed us all that night, I can see how beautiful those scales are, even as clenching fear tightens my throat.

Is this another test? Has Dalachite decided it's my time to die after all? But the creature only stares at me for a moment, then gestures at a high, silver table. On it, piled like small buildings, are stacks of thick, colored bars. Oranges, browns, yellows—it's like a warm-colored rainbow. The familiar, I notice, disappears as I step in and shuts the door behind me.

"They will fill you up," the pink gold creature says once we're alone, its voice a soft hiss. "Provided, of course, your body functions like ours."

"My body 'functions'?"

It's not a term or phrase I've heard before, but I'm thankful for something to take my mind away from the tests and terrors I've been through.

"Yes, functions. Surely you know and understand that all things are a product of what lies inside them. The ever present motion churning to keep those eyes of yours blinking, that mind thinking." The creature's voice is a mix of hisses and growls. It sounds strange in my ears, but then so does everything else on *Cobalt*.

"How does yours function?" I ask.

"I am Bas, an Oratus. As is Sax. We are living weapons," Bas says. "We exist to enforce the laws of the galaxy. To keep it stable, harmonious and peaceful for those who live in it."

"That sounds like a speech."

"It is," Bas laughs, a sort of half hiss, half snort. "Now, sit down. Eat. We can't have our prize specimen dying on us."

I follow Bas' orders. Or rather, try to. The table doesn't have chairs, and it's far too tall for me to eat at. The colored bars sit at the level of my eyes, and I'd have to reach up and over to get to them. I do notice, though, that there are gray-shaded plates in the floor alongside the table. I walk over to them, and glance at Bas, hoping she'll give me the answer.

"Simply sit." Bas provides. "They will rise to greet you at whatever height is most appropriate."

I do so, bend my legs and my knees, as if I'm going to sit down. Something rises from the floor, forms a perfect mold, and pushes me up to meet the table. The nutrient bars are now perfectly positioned for effortless snacking.

"That's neat," I say.

Because it is.

"Try them. When you're done, you can use the facilities there," Bas points to a small door off the kitchen with a green frame.

I devour three of the bars—hunger rising in me at the food, even if it tastes dry and dull, to demand I stuff myself full. After, I use what Bas calls a lavatory, a strange experience where, once again, smooth shaping molds move to accommodate my needs without my asking. Eventually I rejoin Bas at the table, where she hands me a large bowl full of water and bids me to drink.

"You and Sax have strange names," I say after I take a full gulp, with some of the water splashing over the sides onto the table.

Bas doesn't pay any attention to it, so neither do I.

"Stranger still to give them and not receive one in return?" Bas says to me and I blush.

"Kaishi," I say. Bas smiles at me, which, with her rows of sharp teeth, makes me twitch.

Bas watches me take another drink, and when water splashes again, this time bouncing off of the edge of the table onto my clothes —still the cape and robe I've been wearing since we left home—she laughs a second time.

"I usually drink from something smaller?" I ask, nodding at the bowl.

"I'm sorry, Kaishi. It seems *Cobalt* is not ready for your presence," Bas replies, spreading her claws in what I think is a shrug. "I'm sure Dalachite will strive harder in the future to accommodate your species."

It's an admonishment. I can tell that much by her tone. Still, I shelve my pride to ask other, more important questions.

"What is this place?" I ask. "A station? What's Dalachite?"

"A creature you don't know," Bas replies. "If we are the weapons of the galaxy, Dalachite and its brethren are its mind. Amigga run stations like this, control our governments. Lead teams searching for scientific discoveries, and determine what we should do with them."

"You obey them?"

"I enjoy slashing my claws through an enemy, exploring a new world, or diving into a battle to see it won," Bas replies. "The Amigga like none of these things. So we make ideal partners."

"And one of them runs this station?"

"One of them *is* this station. When an Amigga chooses a home, like this one, it's built around them. They are literally embedded inside so that they can see and sense everything. It's why we brought you here."

"So it could study me."

"So it could find a solution," Bas reaches over and rests a claw on my forehead. I should jerk back, but I'm too tired. If this Oratus feels like killing me, I won't have the energy to fight back.

"You mean the thing inside my head. Ignos." I decide to stick with the name. Ignos hasn't offered a new one, and I don't care enough to change it anymore.

"What you carry is the galaxy's greatest enemy, and we will do anything to stop it."

She doesn't know what she's talking about. Her kind, and these Amigga, they are the galaxy's true demons. They rip apart any who think differently, who stand before them. Do not trust them, Kaishi. Do not, or you will wind up their toy to twist and turn and poke and prod until you are nothing.

Bas tilts her head at me. Watches my eyes. "It's talking to you, isn't it?"

I nod.

"Sevora, I know you're listening." Bas is talking to me, and yet not. "Do not harm this one, or I will taste you between my jaws. And I will chew slowly." Her eyes narrow on mine. "As for you, Kaishi, know that you have friends on the station. Those who will protect you."

I'm about to thank her, then I remember that Bas and Sax brought me here, want Dalachite to test me, and I say nothing.

The door opens behind me, the noise saving me from an awkward silence. A familiar stands in it, gesturing at the both of us to stand and follow. Dalachite's voice crackles around us, "A specimen has been wounded. Until the situation is contained, please return to your quarters. Immediately."

26 / WORTH A LIFE

Viera is light in Sax's midclaws. Barely heavier than a furry Flaum. The weight means Sax outruns Malo, leaving the warrior behind as he dashes through the hallways. Dalachite already knows what's happened, and panels in the floor change green in front of Sax to guide him towards *Cobalt*'s medical bay.

When he needs to move, Sax can be very, very fast: His claws bite deep into the floor, leaving scratches but propelling Sax forward in long heaves. His tail catches lips in hallway intersections and pushes Sax in the right direction. Even his foreclaws, empty, grab what they can and push.

All the same, Viera is losing a lot of blood. It splashes and leaves a brutal trail. Sax feels the thick, hot liquid on his skin, and he resists the urge to lick it away. To take a small bite of the specimen so vulnerable in front of him.

His mission is to protect, not destroy.

There are three familiars already in the medical bay when Sax arrives. All of them looking vaguely like humans, or Flaum. Two arms, two legs and at various heights. The number of blue figures stops Sax. It confirms what he fears; that Dalachite has far more familiars running around the station than it's let on thus far. Any or all of them could come after Sax with swords or miners.

But that's not important. Not right now.

What's worse is that *Cobalt* is old, and its treatments outdated. The medical chamber is a single large room with a split bed in the middle. It's large and wide, with thin lines visible where, if necessary, the platform can break apart to hold multiple patients. Right now it's as one, and it's where Sax lays Viera.

As the human body hits the bed, lights above Viera grow bright. Machines and equipment wheel forward from the corners of the room under their own power. They stop at the right length for Viera's mass and width. Programmed to optimal efficiency. Except nothing happens. Viera groans, and the deep gash beneath and to the left of her neck continues to leak.

"We have no protocols," Dalachite says overhead. "There are no standards for this species. No commands to follow."

"It's a carbon-based form. Scan and repair," Sax hisses.

"Why risk damaging the specimen further?" Dalachite replies. "If it dies, then we can still harvest it. We can still learn. Or you can try to save it, ruin it with some ill-conceived attempt. Then what would we get? Nothing."

The mission is protection.

Sax steps forward to the split bed, towers over Viera. There's one common rule when dealing with injuries like this, and that is to stop the bleeding. Then restore fluid and blood, if possible. Sax barks the orders. The familiars don't move, but the machines, programmed to respond to vocal commands, leap to action.

The bed itself flashes blue beneath Viera for a second, running a scan of the human's anatomy. Immediately after, a robotic bundle of thin spindly arms, each with a different tool on the end, bursts into activity. Reaching forward with a dozen different tiny appendages to snip and snap and sew until the gash disappears under a cascade of stitches.

Another mobile rack with various bags of hanging fluids and

drugs, shifts near Viera, adjusts itself and aims a syringe. It stabs Viera's left forearm. The syringe pulls back some of Viera's blood and, like the bed, flashes blue for a microsecond. The bags shift on the rack, one with a deep crimson coming forward and slotting into the tubing leading down to the syringe. Synthetic blood.

It's strange that *Cobalt* would have the necessary fluids for a new species, but Sax is glad of it all the same. Still other robots tend to Viera's needs. They dive down from the ceiling to clip away clothing, to measure heartbeats and breath. To make sure that she's warmed with heated rays from above and below.

Sax watches with the familiars. Old medicine. On a modern ship or station, Viera would be dunked into a bio-tank and regenerated through its mixture of nutrients, nanobots, and living cells ready to substitute for what her body could not do for itself.

Cobalt is an old station, and old methods must suffice.

Malo bursts into the room, finally. Sax notices the warrior is still carrying his sword and, before Malo can make another move, Sax reaches over and tears the weapon from him. Malo barely reacts, his eyes on Viera.

"Alive?" the warrior asks.

"Too soon to tell," Sax replies. "Your attack was good. A clever move."

From the horrified way Malo looks at him, it's clear the warrior can understand Sax, even if he doesn't quite know how to speak in common tongue.

But Sax isn't much of a talker anyway. They settle in. Stare at the buzzing machines.

Watch a human's life creep back from the endless abyss.

27 / THE EMPRESS, ALONE

Bas ignores the familiar, brushing by its blue, protesting arms. She says she knows the way to the medical bay. But after the third turn, after we see our first splotch of dropped blood, two familiars come out of the hallway ahead of us and block the path.

Point us back.

"Both of you to your respective chambers please," Dalachite says. "There's been an accident, and while cleanup is underway I would appreciate it if everyone kept themselves out of this mess."

It isn't a request.

The familiars split Bas and I, the pink-gold Oratus giving me one last wave of her claw as our familiars lead us in different directions. We make our way quick back to the rooms that, I suppose, now, belong to Viera, Malo, and I. Both of theirs, I notice, have glowing red lights above their doorways. Locked, or absent.

I'm shuttled into mine without comment, and the door shuts behind me as soon as I'm inside. It's strange being alone now. The fun mystery and excitement of being somewhere new has worn off. So has the fear. I replace it with grim determination. Acceptance. This isn't where I want to be, but if I'm going to leave, I'm going to escape, and to do that, I first have to stop denying that I'm here at all.

So I look around my room. Try to find something useful. There's the soft, raised bed that is obviously for sleeping. Something which I haven't done since arriving on *Cobalt* and which, my fuzzy brain is telling me, I may need soon.

But not yet.

Elsewhere, other than the blank pearl walls, there's a black screen on one side and a small door that opens to my own... what did Bas call it? Lavatory. I look in there now and notice there's a strange thing in the ceiling in a compartment to the left of where the lavatory's primary business is conducted.

It's a lattice of holes. There's a button on the wall beneath them, that, when I press it, I find it's not just a button but also a dial. If I turn it to the left, it begins to glow red. Turn it right, it glows blue. When I press it in, stale-smelling water sprays down from the holes. I realize the dial, here, controls the temperature: red makes the water hot, blue makes it cold.

I've been chilly since making it to the station, so I take off my ragged cape and enjoy a few, fleeting moments underneath those hot drops. When I press the button again, some time later, I'm blasted with dry air from all angles, from vents with holes so tiny I didn't even notice them before. At the end of it, I'm clean.

I'm about to pull my old clothes back on when I notice, behind the bed, a new cabinet is open. I'm not sure why, whether someone came into my room while I was in the lavatory or if the opening is automatic, but bright blue—like the sky back home—clothes are in there. At least, that's what I think they are, but when I pull the top one from the pile and set it on the bed, it seems to puddle together.

It's a mask.

There's awe in Ignos' words.

I've never actually seen one like this.

But what is it?

The Amigga prefer things activated by touch. So place your hand on it. See what happens.

I do so. Lay my hand flat on the blue... I want to call it fabric, but it's clearly not. Too smooth, too lifeless. Yet when I touch it, like the Cache did so long ago in the jungle, the mask grabs onto my fingers. Pulls itself up my hand, arm, and eventually over my entire body. Even my head. I close my eyes as the mask rushes over them. There's a sense of fleeting pressure, and when it's gone, I open my eyes to clear vision.

I'm suddenly warm. Perfectly so.

When I look down at myself, it's though I'm clothed tight. A form I've never seen before, but one that fits my every angle, and makes me colored silver-blue, like the familiars in bright light. Even my hands appear gloved. Like a Lunare, clothed to stay warm under the mountains.

The thought interrupts my fascination like the crack of Viera's pistol.

One of my friends is hurt, and here I am, playing in my room. Forgetting all about them.

If you want to learn what's happened, use the console.

I stare at the screen on the wall to the left of the door. It's blank and dark.

Remember, Kaishi? Place your hand on it.

I do so, laying my right hand flat against the screen. It leaves an impression, and when a leaf-green line begins to outline my fingertips against the screen, I jerk it back. The illustration vanishes.

Leave it there. It needs to know who you are.

I stare at my hand for second. Who I am? How is this thing going to know from my hand, who I am?

It looks for signals. Etchings in your palm, the heat of your hand. The mask gives you to it. That's how the console knows it's you and not Malo. Whether you're an Oratus or an Amigga.

I still don't quite understand, but I press my hand again to the screen. Once the green tracing finishes, the black fades away to a soft white background similar but not quite matching the tone of the walls. Against it are colorful symbols. One is a shifting spiral. The other appears to be a circle suspended in an oval shape. Another is a jumble of letters mashed into a square, and so on and so forth they go. There must be dozens of them.

A knock interrupts my exploration. This time, when I look towards the door, the light flashes green and the door parts to reveal Malo on the other side.

Only it's not the Malo I remember. This one, my friend, is covered in blood. He holds a crumpled up set of clothes in his arms. I know the uniform. The robe. Viera's.

"Is she alive?" I ask, and when Malo nods, I sigh in relief.

"I nearly killed her, Kaishi," Malo says as he enters the room. He holds out the clothes as if I'm supposed to take them. As if they're mine now, somehow.

"How?" I reply, and Malo tells me.

"It was for my people," Malo says at the end of his story. "At least, that's what I thought. She mocked us. The Charre. But what are mere words in a place like this? When all we have is each other?"

Malo's face is the picture of anguish. He sits on the side of my bed and stares at the console, though I don't think he sees it. "Do you know why we were out in the jungle, raiding Solare tribes?" Malo's not expecting me to answer, so I don't. "Because we wanted to know what the Lunare were doing. We wanted to know what they wanted from you so that we could get it first."

"To keep them from having it?" I say.

"No. So that we could try to buy a better life for us. From them." He leans forward, presses his hands against his knees, then forces his eyes to me. "You saw what they brought to the field. You saw those strange creatures. The rolling machines of war. They were going to crush us, Kaishi. Wipe us away if we stood in front of them. So I was searching for a way out. A way to save our people, and I found one."

"You found a lie."

"Be that as it may, it worked. Now I'm here, but I don't think the wounds are closed. I lost myself in my hate, Kaishi. Which is less than you deserve. I'm not worthy of you, of serving you or my people."

Malo rises suddenly. Brushes by me as if he's going to leave.

"Am I still your Empress?" I say.

There's a long heartbeat.

"You are my Empress," Malo replies, facing the door.

"Then as your Empress, I command you to stay. To help me and Viera. To be my sword when I need it, and my shield when I don't. Do you accept?"

Malo stiffens, but there is no hesitation.

"I accept, Empress."

Without another word, Malo strides from the room. The door shuts behind him.

I'm left alone with Viera's bloody clothes.

28 / WHEN PUSH COMES TO CLAW

Bas comes into the med bay covered in a destroyed familiar's blue spatter. Sax takes one look at the evidence and bares a toothy grin.

"It tried to keep me away from you," Bas explains. "It failed."

On the table in the middle is the human. Still being monitored, still being worked on, though the intensity of the machines dies down as Viera gets further and further away from losing her life. The three familiars stay, staring at the human, and so Sax and Bas will stay too.

"The Amigga wants to let her die," Sax says. "Take her for parts."

Bas does a slow pan through the room. "Not a terrible plan."

"I put her in this mess. A training accident. Not the way for a warrior to go." Sax clicks his claws against each other. "Besides, I thought we wanted them alive?"

"Insofar as they serve our needs," Bas replies and then goes on to relay the details of meeting Kaishi. How she thinks the human is definitely not captive to the Sevora and may actually be coming to hate the thing inside her mind. "She smells of sadness. Not quite despair, but not far from it."

"She needs an objective," Sax says. "Something to aim at. Something worth living for."

They both turn back to the human on the bed.

"Do you think they pair like we do?" Bas asks.

"That one mentioned something like it. It sounded awful."

"You can't judge other species by the greatness of your own, Sax."

Yet, Sax feels he can. It's justified, in fact. For how else can Sax measure who he is, what he is, without benchmarks? Without seeing just how far below him everything else is?

The predator must know his prey.

"I need to send a message to Evva," Sax says after several minutes of buzzing medical machines. "She needs to know what we think."

Bas is about to reply when the three familiars turn as one and look at them. "You disobeyed me." Dalachite's voice comes from above. "You shattered another of my familiars."

"It was fun," Bas says. "And it can remake itself."

"Not if you walk away wearing it," the Amigga continues. "When I ask you to return to your quarters, I expect you to do so. This is my station and you will follow my requests."

"Those requests sound more like orders," Sax says.

Without really thinking about it, he and Bas separate by a meter. Enough room to maneuver should the three familiars get some idea. Though they're all unarmed, and Sax still holds the sword Malo brought with him. If any fight breaks out, winning would be quick and easy.

"Call it what you want, so long as you obey," Dalachite says. "But it's time, I think, to rest. This one's life is well in hand. She's breathing, her heart is beating."

"How do we know you won't kill her as soon as we leave the room?" Sax replies.

"Because I'm not a monster," Dalachite says. "Besides, I can learn as much by watching this one heal as I can by killing her. See how her cellular structure reforms. What her body does to combat potential infections. All you've done is change the parameters of my studies. Not ruin them."

"Do we trust it?" Sax asks his pair.

"I'm not sure we have a choice, unless we intend to fight every familiar on the station." Bas waves a claw at the three blue creatures in front of them. "Let's go. I'm tired as it is."

They leave the med bay. Head back towards their quarters, except halfway there, Sax pulls off. Goes towards the docking bay. When Dalachite asks why, Sax says that they left a number of supplies on the shuttle. The excuse pays off, and Dalachite doesn't talk anymore. It's a quiet walk the rest of the way.

Sax acts normal as he goes up the boarding ramp. Heads to the bridge, where the console and transmitter lie. There's no way to cover what he's doing here, so Sax has to hope Dalachite is busy with other tasks and isn't watching through the windshield.

Staring at the bay's bright green light beyond the glass, Sax presses the button to record and begins to speak. He leaves a long message; shares what's happened on the station. Explains how he believes Dalachite is threatening him. That Sax thinks this will fall apart sooner rather than later.

When the transmission ends, Sax leaves the bridge. Grabs a token crate of nutrient bars. Heads back through the twisting hallways, towards the quarters. Makes it to the last one when Dalachite finally speaks.

"Suspiciously few supplies, Oratus," the Amigga says.

"Had a craving for our own food. But tell me, Amigga, do you ever sleep?" Sax replies. "Are you always spying?"

"Always spying, Oratus. Always seeing."

"Then I hope what you saw met your expectations," Sax says.

There are any of a dozen formal goodbyes. Ways to say good evening and good night. Sax uses none of them. None are worthy of this encounter. None are worth dispensing on Dalachite and its blue creatures.

Bas already has her mask off and is lying on the large soft sponge that serves as an Oratus bed. Their limbs tangle with each other on the reddish, soft surface. The sponge is cool to the touch, and it bends and folds around them. Their claws puncture it, but it heals around their points so Sax feels surrounded by a thick glove.

As they do every time they sleep together, Sax sends his tail out along the base of the sponge where it meets Bas'. They wrap around each other, and their claws dig through the sponge to clasp.

And the pair sleeps.

29 / HISTORIES

I'm sitting on the bed. Wearing the mask and wondering how to take it off. It doesn't seem right to sleep in such a thing, not that it isn't comfortable, but I feel as though it's monitoring me. Measuring what and who I am every second and modulating appropriately. It's a strange feeling, and not one that will lend itself to dreams. Dreams I think will already be hard in coming, considering where I am.

I believe you can take it off.

I ask how and Ignos doesn't reply. Apparently it doesn't know. I glance at the Cache, still tight on my wrist. Again I see a bright green flash and it's as though I'm in a giant forest of information. Pictures hover in my mind's eye, and the Cache attempts to search for what I'm thinking about: the mask. All it finds, though, are fuzzy descriptions. Hunches and speculations about how they work.

While I'm in, I focus on the term 'Amigga' and the Cache obliges. No pictures—apparently, whatever created the Cache hasn't ever seen an Amigga in the flesh—but plenty of text. It's full of adjectives: scientific, aggressive, impersonal and focused. There's a curious sentence about the Amigga having more to do with the current state of the galaxy than any other species, but, when I try to dig further, the Cache comes up empty.

So I blink it away and turn to the only other thing in my room that might hold answers: the console. Its screen is still on. Full of those dizzying icons. Ignos wakes up and begins explaining them to me. I focus on the knowledge databases, like the Cache. Using one, I pull up a map of *Cobalt* and look at where the medical bay is, where my platform room stands. Memorize what I can of it, even though half the terms are unknown to me.

I pay particular attention to the route from my room to the docking bay. To our escape.

From there, an icon that looks like a spinning circle with numbers and dashes catches my attention. I tap it and see a log of events. Simple, laid out one after the other to the dates themselves, all aligned under what the log call "cycles". The log shows ten of them.

A cycle can last a long time, depending on what happens. Hundreds and thousands of your Earth years might pass from one to the next. Or only a dozen.

Dalachite built *Cobalt* in the eighth cycle. Deliberately at distance from the rest of the galaxy—a term I don't understand.

You and all your tribes are but an infinitesimal part of everything, Kaishi. Yet, you may be the most important discovery since the beginning of the cycles.

Because of Ignos, or so that's what Bas said.

Yes.

There's a small burst of frustration from Ignos then, as if the admission pains it somehow. Nothing I can do about it, though, so I look back at the timeline.

Cobalt, after completion, went along at first without anything noted. Tests were assigned and completed. Staff stayed and morale reports showed that things were happy. All recorded in brief, bland updates. The first blip occurs not long after the station was built. When half the staff departed the station. There's a short note indicating the scientists were superfluous and were removed to decrease supply expenses. From then on, every entry marks more and more scientists departing. The notes, though, change to indicate the removals were due to increased efficiency.

The mystery isn't hard to solve: the familiars slowly replaced everyone. I glide over the remaining notes of staff departures and successful experiments, until I come to the very last one:

The last of us are leaving, not through our own desires, as we have spent all our lives here, but because Dalachite has decided we are no longer relevant. Its blue 'familiars' are everywhere now, watching our every move, haunting our footsteps. We Sevora may not match the Amigga's intelligence, but we are living beings; we have souls, we have dreams and desires. The familiars have none of these. That Dalachite finds this an advantage is obvious.

One is opening the door even now.

I bid you goodbye, Cobalt, and may your master drown in the void of its creations.

I tap away from the timeline. The only thing on this station, then, are the three of us, Sax and Bas, Dalachite and its familiars. Elsewhere on the console I find, finally, instructions on how to remove the mask. The creature that appears on the screen to demonstrate makes me stumble back; it looks like a tall, brown-furred mouse with a longer, naked nose. Yet it's clear what its small claws are doing. So I try it.

I spread the fingers in my hands, then press them down against my own palms. It feels like stepping out of the shower; the mask slides off me and clusters on the floor in a bundle like when I first found it. I set it aside, crawl into bed. Say the words that make the lights go out.

A second later I turn those lights back on. The darkness without them is absolute. Total. Like in the chamber with the platform. My heart races. Chills and sweats mingle across my body. I take a few seconds. Long deep breaths.

You can dim them.

I say the words Ignos tells me, and rather than vanishing, the lights quiet to the level of dying twilight. A soft, orange glow. Low enough for me to sleep, bright enough to keep from triggering my fears.

Though I wonder why Ignos keeps helping me.

Because you are still my only way to survive.

How can I trust it?

You have to choose to. I can't make you. But I will always try to help you. Because without you, I am nothing.

I have to trust Ignos won't hurt me. I can't get it out of my head anyway. It's with that knowledge that I fall asleep. Slowly, waiting for dreams and nightmares.

30 / WEAPONS TESTING

The nutrient bars are the same this morning as they were the day before. Not that days have any real meaning on *Cobalt*—the lights here shift to simulate day and night, but there aren't seasons, calendars to keep track of.

Sax is grateful for the protein. For the energy. Especially when the familiars show up again. They look at him, at Bas with their blank blue faces. There are two of them this time, and when they point to Sax, he's not surprised.

"Another exercise?" Dalachite says. "I've made some adjustments. I think you'll find it more interesting this time."

If there's any lingering animosity from yesterday's events, Sax doesn't hear it. As if the Amigga has moved on, chalked it up as a squabble not worth mentioning. Sax is fine with that. He's made his transmission to Evva, and there's plenty of weapons for the Oratus in their quarters. If things get worse, they'll be ready.

"Do you want me to go this time?" Bas says.

"I would much prefer him," Dalachite interrupts. "I'm calibrating the familiars, and so I need a consistent source subject. One whose styles I can analyze and then see how effective my tweaks have been."

"What kind of tweaks?" Sax asks.

"It would ruin the purpose of the demonstration were I to tell you ahead of time. The whole exercise lies in how well they, and you, adapt."

Sax, beneath the table, sneaks his tail beneath Bas and delivers two quick taps to the bottom of her own tail. He stands up, looks at the two familiars. "Fine. Now that I've got a full stomach, you'll have all the advantage you need."

"To win?" Dalachite laughs.

"Oh, you'll lose," Sax replies. "Just more slowly."

The two familiars lead him through the hallways and back to the same training room. It bears the scars from Sax's gunplay the night before, burns Dalachite does not acknowledge. This time the two familiars go to the center of the room and turn back to Sax.

"Another chase, like yesterday?" Sax asks.

"I think it would be the perfect place to start," Dalachite says. "Whenever you're ready."

This time the familiars don't even move. They stand there, watch Sax. He looks at them. Both familiars are the same size. Both have the same two legs and arms. Neither one capable of outrunning an Oratus. Neither one wearing any sort of weapon. How is this going to be any different than before?

Not that it matters. Sax bares his teeth, clenches his legs, fakes towards the one on the left, and then lunges at the one to the right.

His clawed feet pump into long leaps, and Sax catches the familiar with his midclaws, cuts it to pieces. The familiar explodes in a tremendous blue spray.

Something bites Sax's back. A micro stunner's tingling burn. If Sax wasn't wearing a mask, he'd be in a lot more pain. As it is, the spot in the middle of his spine feels like a lit candle is being held up to it.

"So you're cheating today," Dalachite says as Sax whirls around to see the other familiar. Rather than running to the wall as it did on the day before, the familiar sprinted right to the cabinet. Cut behind Sax after the Oratus went right, and armed itself.

"You're one to talk," Sax roars. The micro-stunner could damage the mask, if Sax let it. "You said this was a chase. Not an attack."

"The battlefield changes constantly, Oratus."

The familiar fires again. The bolt strikes Sax in the chest, burning, but otherwise dispersing through the mask's defenses.

If that's how the Amigga wants it, then Sax will play its game. He darts towards the second familiar, this time using his feet to dance to the right. Towards the door and the wall around it. The familiar tracks and fires another shot. This one misses. A little too slow. Sax angles slightly left, jumps, uses the gravity to hit the padding above the door and spring off so that he's flying towards the familiar at a diagonal angle.

The familiar can't get the miner aimed quickly enough and Sax smashes it, presses the familiar back against the cabinet where his claws rend it into goo.

Any taste of victory dies when Sax hears the door open behind him. Turns to see four more familiars walk in. These are not empty-handed. Each one holds another sword. Not an old model from the cabinet either. These are newer. They shine with circuitry. With buzzing edges. Made to cut right through metal, or through a mask.

"Well done, Oratus. You've exceeded my expectations. However, you've also tried to undermine my station with your little message. I'm sorry, but our experiments are over."

Sax reaches behind him, pulls a pair of miners from the cabinet. The broken ones from before. He takes a quick glance back, sees the working one that he used with Malo and Viera, but it hasn't been recharged. There's one sword still left though. So he takes that. The four familiars advance slowly, each one holding its blade in front of it, level towards the Oratus.

Sax sinks to a crouch, drops the broken rifles and holds the sword in his left foreclaw. The four familiars march in a line, which means the ends are the weak spots. Sax doesn't want to get trapped against a wall, so he feints to the right. Away from the familiars and towards space. Then he uses his tail, grabbing the inside of the cabinet, to yank himself back left. Sax claws the up the wall and jumps. He's not going for an attack this time and soars high over the row of blue heads.

The familiars all turn to follow him as Sax lands on the far end of the room, plenty of clear padding between him and his enemies. As Sax hits the ground he bursts forward, charging right at the center of the line. His legs and midclaws scramble on the ground, pushing faster across the room. The four familiars prepare their swings. Sax rolls. His right claws bite into the padding hard. Pull Sax towards the door. Towards that side of the line and out of the range of the two left familiars swinging down towards where he should have been.

As Sax spins, his tail lashes over his shoulders to catch the head of the closest familiar, the one on the end of the right side. The blow doesn't break it, but sends the familiar reeling back.

Buys Sax a second.

Which is all he needs.

Sax completes the roll, he catches himself on his legs and darts forward at the next familiar. Its blade sweeps to meet him, and Sax catches it with his own. But where the familiar only has one weapon, Sax has many. He presses the familiar's blade up and sweeps beneath it with his midclaws.

The familiar breaks apart, and as Sax's skin is pelted with blue goop, he catches its buzzing sword with his tail as it falls to the ground, and flips it at the next familiar. The sword spins end over end, slicing right through the familiar's liquid middle. Which leaves only two.

No, four. Sax counts quick. The other two are back near the cabinet. The ones Sax tore apart earlier. They're grabbing the small, stunning miners.

So that's it then. Sax sees it all in an instant. The familiars putting themselves back together. They'll keep coming, keep hacking away at him until Sax inevitably makes a mistake. Until he gets too tired, or simply misses something.

He notices a red glow above the only exit.

Sax won't leave this room alive.

31 / THE GRAND DESIGN

The opening door shocks me awake. The lights rise from their dim glow to bright scalding white, and as my eyes come into focus I see the blank head of a blue familiar standing there. Staring at me, or at least I think so, though I can't see its eyes.

"Time for our next session," Dalachite's voice says.

I get out of the bed and the familiar watches me as I put on the mask. It's the only clothes I have now, and the mask feels better than my old robe and cape. Fewer scratches, less dirt. It warms me up to the perfect temperature. The mask is also, aside from the Cache, the only real possession I have. It's a comfort to have it close.

I follow the familiar down the hallway, noticing that both Malo and Viera's doors are red-locked. I don't even know if Viera is out of the med bay, and when I ask I receive no response. Part of me wants to stay back, to resist the familiar just to see what would happen, but Ignos tells me not to.

Making Dalachite angry is only going to hurt you more.

This time we go to a different room. There's no platform, no spherical wall, but instead a single long shelf on one side and, on it, a tank full of greenish water. There's nothing else in the room, though I can see some scuffing on the floor. As if furniture had been here at one point, and now moved. There's another familiar in the room, near the tank. It waves me over. As I go, the familiar that led me shuts the door and, I notice, moves to stand in front of it.

I know what's going to happen.

I don't.

When it does, I want you to remember that I'm on your side. Remember that I want the best for the both of us.

I know that. I don't necessarily believe it, but I trust it when Ignos says that its own survival depends on me. It's in my head after all, so if Dalachite decides now is my time to die, it seems likely Ignos would go with me.

I get near the tank. The familiar directs me to the center so that I'm staring across the water. The tank itself is about a meter wide and nearly half a meter deep. There's nothing in it, aside from the liquid. I don't see fish or anything swimming, no plants growing.

The familiar shoves me in.

Not all of me. Just my face and my head. The familiar holds me down and pushes me beneath the surface. I start to shout, to scream, but then I realize I don't need to. I'm still able to breathe, and it's not hard to know why. The mask. It's doing the work for me. So I stop struggling and wait to see what's going to happen next.

I don't have to wait long. The familiar holding me down doesn't relax his grip, but, through the blurred walls of the tank, I see the other familiar come close. He reaches beneath the shelf, and comes back with a shiny silver device almost as long as my arm.

This may hurt Kaishi, but it will be worse for me than for you.

The familiar reaches over with the device, pushes it beneath the water. I feel the ripples as it comes close and I know exactly where it's going. Now I struggle; my hands and arms jerk. I try to kick with my legs, but the familiars are strong. Stronger than me, anyway, and they ignore my attempts.

Stop it, Kaishi. They will only hurt you.

They're going to do that anyway. Ignos, though, is insistent, sad.

So I let myself relax. Shut my eyes. Feel the silver piece slide into my ear. The mask coats my skin, but there's something about the device. Something that makes the mask recoil and creates a hole. Ignos starts to tell me, and I catch the word electric, before all is lost.

Before, in the first session, I felt it when Ignos experienced pain. When it thrashed and turned and writhed in my mind. This is similar, only not so random. It's as though Ignos is caught in a net. Stuck on the end of something, and the thrashes are focused. They prickle the right side of my head and my temple burns, and then I feel it. A rushing, slimy thing, leaving tiny scratches across my ear as it moves.

There's a sudden pop. A vacuum. My ears clearing and then I'm being pulled back. Out of the water and away from the tank.

"Look at it," Dalachite's voice comes into the room.

The Amigga doesn't have to tell me, because I can't look away. In the tank is something both small and terrifyingly large. A narrow, sloping body nearly transparent, so that I can see the small batch of organs inside. The very top seems to fray into a thousand strands: long, stringy things that stretch out through the tank as the water shifts. That drift all the way to the edges.

"That is a Sevora," Dalachite says. "That is what is inside you. What is telling you the things that you should do. That is whose demands you've been following."

The thing about nightmares is that they're often scarier when you can't see them. When they travel through the shades of dreams waiting to spring upon you, and you know that they're there but you don't know what they are. Here though, here I'm seeing Ignos in the flesh. I'm seeing the thing that was inside me.

I know then that when I slipped into the black ink in the jungle, this came into my mind.

"There's something very special about your species Kaishi," Dalachite says. "Something that we have not seen before. Something the Sevora did not expect. Do you see all those fronds there? They wrap and ensnare your nerves. They splice into all that you are and take you. Twist you and turn you into a puppet. But this didn't happen with you, did it?"

"I could hear it. We could talk to each other."

I remember of course. I remember after I woke up. With Ignos in my head. When it complained about how it couldn't move me. How I couldn't move my own legs until it gave the control back. Why?

"That is why the Sevora are the enemy of the galaxy," Dalachite continues. "They take intelligent races and subvert them to their own ends. A true evil. A parasite. You, and the rest of your species, may hold the secret to preventing that."

"What secret?"

"Somewhere in that body of yours is the reason that Sevora is unable to take you over as it would any other species. It's my job to find out what that is."

I'm afraid to ask but I do anyway. "How?"

There's no answer, at least not a verbal one. But I find out soon enough. The familiars take hold of me again and bring me back to the tank. Press me under the water. My eyes are open and I watch, they even let me tilt my head enough to see the Sevora. To see Ignos.

It doesn't swim so much as bob, until the strands flutter. They move as one, waving back and forth and pushing the Sevora towards me.

When Ignos touches my head, I feel its stringy tentacles. They press against the mask and then bounce away. The Sevora can't, doesn't try to go back inside. But instead it sits there, hovering near my head.

I should be horrified, I suppose. Should be screaming or panicking. I'm not. Partly because, I think, I know it's Ignos there. I know that it's had so many opportunities to hurt me and hasn't. Not directly, anyway. I also have no choice. I can't fight these familiars.

Not alone.

Part of me, too, is curious. The silver thing comes back into the water, guided by a familiar's hand, and approaches my ear. This time, when it punctures the mask, I can feel it moving around, almost touching the sides of my skin. The mask recoils from it, and the space gives the Sevora a chance to shoot forward into my ear like an arrow. The trailing edges of its tentacles crawl once more into my mind.

Into me.

This time, I know what to look for. I feel a second consciousness tap into mine. The tingle in my nerves as they say they're no longer sending messages just to me. When my head pulls out of the water moments later, I hear Ignos.

I'm sorry, Kaishi.

32 / ATTRITION

He's never going to be able to beat these things.

Sax runs around the room, jumping and leaping and rolling. Making precise moves when he needs to take out the two familiars that keep trying to get the micro-stunners. The four with the swords chase, but they're slow. Sloppy.

Sax is going to get sloppy too. His muscles are already burning. His mask bears scorch marks from near misses. He's going to make a mistake and die beneath a familiar's blade.

How is he going to get out of here?

Sax takes another flying leap up the wall and then jumps onto the ceiling, latching on with his claws. The familiars with the swords head to the sides and begin their weird suction run up towards him. Sax has only seconds to breathe. Meanwhile the two stunner-wielding familiars are reassembling themselves from the latest thrashing. There's nothing else in the room, except the glowing red light over the door.

The door.

It's metal, too strong for Sax to break through with his claws alone. There's more than claws in this room, however. More than micro-stunners and swords. He glances at the cabinet. The one miner still in there. Half-charged from his show time with Malo and Viera, but even half should be enough to blow a hole in the door. Weaken it for Sax to get through.

Now that he has a plan, Sax wastes no time. He skitters along the ceiling, towards a sword-wielder reaching the top of the wall and turning upside down. Sax meets him, and as the familiar swings his sword, the Oratus bursts forward. Sax gets beneath the strike and slams the familiar into the wall. They both fall, the low gravity and padded floor letting Sax hit the bottom without injury, though his claws mean the familiar can't say the same.

The other sword-wielders drop themselves, and while they're doing that, Sax gets a free run at the cabinet. Jerks it open, grabs a rifle and turns face-to-face with a pair of micro-stunners. They fire, and the two blasts catch Sax right in the chest. The stunners burn, searing hot and a strange wave of numbness spreads.

He can't give up now or he'll get hacked to pieces.

There's a thing that happens with Oratus. When they're desperate, angry, when they're fighting for their lives. Sax calls it the bloodlust, and it wraps him up in fury now. Pushes away the burns, the aches, the exhaustion. Sax surges, takes another two blasts and then he's through the familiars. Bashing them to the ground and throwing the stunners across the room.

A pair of sword-wielders is next, and Sax sidesteps them. Does a quick jump towards the center of the room and swings in the air. He aims the miner at the door. Pulls the trigger as he floats and unleashes a lance of azure energy that strikes its target. The door's center-right side glows orange before curling and blackening away from the beam, which sputters out a moment later.

Older miners suck power like a Fassoth sucks food. Sax has forgotten how many power packs they used to carry.

The third sword-wielder catches Sax from behind, nearly lops off his tail, but Sax feels the air moving as the sword comes and only suffers a gash instead. The Oratus turns and, with a single bite, obliterates the familiar's head. Swallows the goop. Sax isn't sure if it'll make him sick, but he knows the stuff won't be going back to reform the thing.

The two swords that he had dodged are closing in. They stand between Sax and the door, but Sax doesn't have time for this. He turns the miner sideways and whips it at the right swordsman. The familiar moves to block, but Sax follows his own toss with a leaping jump. Catches the rifle as the swordsman blocks, and uses the added momentum to shove the blade back into the swordsman's own body.

Sax bowls it over and continues towards the door. The last swordsman turns to give chase, but it's too slow. Sax barrels into the weakened door, which blows apart as the Oratus hammers into it. Sax rolls into the hallway, scrambles on the floor and launches himself down the corridor. He hears Dalachite's voice. Calling to him, laughing at him. Ordering him back to the room.

Sax ignores the sounds of his prey.

He heads towards his quarters. This time there are no green lights telling him where to go. No familiars pointing the right direction. Sax homes in on one thing and one thing only: the smell of his pair. The scent of her guides him through the station, and when he opens the door to their quarters, he finds Bas already armed. She takes one look at the gash on Sax's tail and the burn marks covering his skin and hisses. It's not a laugh, it's not a greeting. A low, angry, fiery rush of air snarling out between her teeth, lips, and the vents lining her chest. A sound Sax has only heard a few times before, a sound reserved for him and those who dare cross her path.

"I'm going to kill it," Sax answers.

"We're going to kill it," Bas replies.

"Secure the specimens," Sax argues. "Secure the shuttle. Make sure we can get off the station."

"You want this, don't you?"

She knows him so well.

"I need this," Sax says.

The prey has been annoying him since they landed here. The familiars are strange abominations. Unnatural. Now Sax can act on it. He gets to put this high and mighty slime into its place. His eyes move to the locker above the bed. There lie a pair of small rifles, and the black bar swords that he prefers.

The Amigga began the fight. Sax will end it.

33 / UNSTEADY

I'm walking back to my room when my two-familiar escort pushes me forward with more urgency. There's no answer to my startled ask, no explanation for being shoved through the halls. Pressed through doors that shut behind us, closing off passages as we pass through them. I wind up back at my room. No chance for food, drink or anything else. The door closes and I hear the familiars pad away.

Something's wrong.

I gather that much. What's more concerning is that the console is dark and doesn't react when I press it. I'd hoped it might have some information on what's happening in *Cobalt*, but no luck. Left without options, the curious furor dies away, which turns my attention to my own head, and what's inside it.

Do you find me disgusting?

Yes. There's no other answer. Not only does Ignos look terrifying, it's inside me. Always there. I now know those long skinny tendrils are wrapping themselves around my body and connecting to my nerves. How am I not supposed to be disgusted? How am I not supposed to be scared?

Knowledge, Kaishi, is the antidote to fear. You fear me because you don't understand what I am. Let me change that.

I don't protest, so Ignos goes on. Tells me the Sevora's story.

The Sevora woke in the distant past. Ignos doesn't know how many cycles ago, and as I don't really comprehend what a cycle is, I don't press it. All it knows is that they exist deep in the caves and caverns of a rocky world. One covered with marshland on the surface.

The Sevora there swam through the waters, occasionally finding and devouring creatures that shared their space. Some grew to full maturity, and embedded themselves on the ground beneath the vast oceans and swamps and birthed new generations. Ignos itself has never reached that stage. Will never, if it has any choice.

Because once you mature, once you burst forth the next generation, you die a long death.

Not really though. Ignos and I have different definitions of death. For it, for most Sevora, death means the loss of new life.

After a Sevora matures, it can no longer take a new host. To travel and to see what else the galaxy holds. Mature Sevora grow into their home. Like Dalachite and this space station. Once the maturation cycle triggers, everything else stops.

I pester Ignos to get back to the story. As interesting as Sevora biology is, I don't need more nightmares. I won't be sleeping as it is.

Ignos heads back to the timeline, to the first instant the Sevora had any inkling of their true abilities. The moment came when intelligent life first visited the planet. A flash in the sky similar to what I experienced back home.

A ship crashed in a shallow swamp. Bands of furry creatures, ones Ignos calls Flaum, emerged. The same ones that I'd seen in the console's videos of how to put on a mask. They stumbled around the swamp, unsure of where they were, and the Sevora took advantage. Stole one, then the next and the next until the entire ship had been made captive. For the first time the Sevora had thumbs and fingers, and ideas for them to steal. They took that knowledge, they took the crashed ship and made more.

And spread.

Their growth happened unheeded for a long time. Ignos is boasting at this point. Diving into a lustful, wistful history that makes it clear this is what Ignos wants to return to. The Sevora infiltrated societies, cities, whole planets and grew to enslave them all. Taking each and every sentient creature's mind and turning it to their collective will.

Until the Amigga found them. Sent the Vincere to carve them back. Since that point it's been a continuous, bloody conflict. The Sevora, however, need captives. Need bodies to host. The Amigga and Oratus, along with all other species, don't have that problem. The lopsided numbers mean the Sevora have been in gradual retreat since the start, and now they're almost gone.

Ignos is looking for sympathy, but, as a Solare that's experienced my people's own decline, I don't have any to spare. Doesn't help that the Sevora live by using others. I'm repulsed by the thought of being a guest in my own body. Hard to get motivated to help a species like that.

Yes, we use species. We take their ideas and expand on them. Enhance their technology, purify their societies of problems both physical and cultural. We stop violence, Kaishi. Crime. Hate. It all goes away. No Sevora, no host starves or wants for medical attention.

I think we can have that without losing freedom.

Then show me where.

I can't. Yet.

Ignos doesn't give up, though.

You and I are connected to the same nerves. If I feel pain, you feel pain. If I feel pleasure, so do you. The species we take, they live and continue to live great lives. It's like watching something on a console, but experiencing the joys of it. The successes. There's no failure, there's no death.

Then why are we here on this station, if the Sevora are so wonderful?

My question goes unanswered for a moment. Ignos eventually comes back slow. Cautious.

We are here because the galaxy does not understand us. Because it sees us as a threat. As enslavers, rather than liberators.

What am I then? How does Ignos see me, someone whose will, whose mind it can't take?

An anomaly. But also, perhaps, an answer. You present a choice to the galaxy, Kaishi. You present the hope of an equilibrium. If we could give the option to a species, the choice of a life lived without stress or fear or worry, or one with all those things but with true freedom? Then perhaps the Sevora would not be hated quite so much.

I don't see how anyone could choose the former, but Ignos laughs.

You've seen the Pits of Damantum, the desperate person who wishes for something better. Who is at the very end of all of their dreams. Who, given the choice would abandon what little their freedom has given them and instead choose comfort, happiness, peace.

I'm about to continue the conversation when there's a knock. My mask lets me connect with the door and shunt it open. Malo's standing outside, his cape and robe torn and ragged, but I'm drawn to Viera, hanging on Malo's shoulder, tired, pale, yet still launching a sharp grin my way.

I can't help it. I scream a little in delight, run forward and hug the Lunare, then the Charre. Tight. Both Malo and Viera return the squeeze, and when I step back, they both look at each other, then at me with small smiles.

"I apologized," says Malo in Charre tongue. "Viera says I'm better with a sword than she expected."

"You're lucky," Viera adds. "Do that thing again and you'll wind up with my blade in your side."

Malo shakes his head, looks at me. "What I've learned, painfully, is that it's just us here. No matter how terrible Viera might be, it's better to have her than to lose her."

"Come in," I say. Partly because I've noticed, in the hallway, there are two familiars standing at the end of our section. They're watching us with their blank blue faces, and it's causing twitchy chills.

Malo and Viera step inside and the door shuts behind them. I keep the conversation in Charre, hoping Dalachite can't make sense of what we're saying.

"Tell me," I speak to Viera. "Tell me what it was like?"

"Unpleasant. A sharp pain, and unconsciousness, and then the slow-growing sensation of a thousand things happening to me. I flickered in and out what must've been a dozen times. Imagine opening your eyes and seeing strange metal limbs coming towards you, pulling back, poking and prodding your skin. Looking to the left and seeing a tube leading from your arm to a strange bag full of red fluid. I'll have nightmares about this forever."

"She showed up at my door," Malo says. "Moments ago. Like this."

"The familiars brought me. They said I should get some rest, but since when have I followed orders?"

"Certainly not mine," I say.

"Obviously. I'm your adviser, not your servant." Viera clicks her teeth. "And as your adviser, I'm wondering, when do we get out of here?"

It's a question I've been pondering since the first session. At once I'm fascinated by everything around me. I want to know more, to understand and grow into this wide universe, but I'm getting the feeling that every moment on this station puts me at risk. Dalachite doesn't, after all, seem all that interested in my health, which makes my answer easy.

"As soon as possible. I don't think Dalachite is going to let us leave alive."

I tell them about my sessions. I tell them about Ignos. They're stunned, but Viera is the quickest to shed her astonishment.

"There's a creature in your mind that's played off as a god? Can't say I'm surprised given what we've seen. Doesn't matter anyway, its answers still worked. Its machines did what they should do. So long as its in your head and not mine, lets use it."

My eyes flick to Malo, to see how he's taking it.

"You're still my empress," Malo replies, bowing his head. "There's more to that than having a god in your head."

Not exactly satisfying, but I'll take it.

"Here's what we need to do," I say. "Get out of here. Find a way to the docking bay, and then I can use the Cache, and Ignos, to learn how to pilot the shuttle."

"You think that thing will let us walk out of here?" Viera asks. "Because I'm betting it'd rather have us chopped up to bits so it can study every one of our insides."

You need weapons.

I pose Ignos' dilemma to the pair.

"The training room," Malo says. "There is a whole cabinet full. I'm sure we could use some of them."

"Because that's what I want, you holding a sword again." Viera says.

"What if I promise to only attack our enemies? Cut up those blue things?"

"I'd be okay with that. So long as I'm at a distance."

I look at both of them. They nod back at me. The plan is set.

We're getting off this station.

34 / EXPERIMENTS

It doesn't take Sax long to encounter the first sign of resistance. Only a few steps out from their quarters, with Bas heading in the opposite direction, and Sax sees a familiar move in front of him from another hallway. It's unarmed; hands by its sides. Sax, with deadly weapons encircling his waist and embedded in the mask, keeps on moving. *Cobalt*'s a large station, it'll be a long hike to get to the center.

"Please," Dalachite's voice pours into the hallway. "Before you come to kill me. Before you decide to end all that this station has been built for, I'd like to show you something."

"You've shown me plenty already," Sax hisses.

The familiar doesn't move, so when Sax is close, he opens his mouth. Makes sure that wherever Dalachite is watching from, it can see those teeth. See what will be tearing through his creation.

"Not this. You haven't seen this before, I guarantee you." What stops Sax is the Amigga's voice. Not the words that it says. But rather the tone.

There's no worry in it. No fear. Only a sly, tantalizing tilt.

"What?" Sax can't resist.

"Follow." Dalachite doesn't say anything else, and the familiar turns and heads down the hallway, in the same direction Sax was going anyway.

Sax follows.

They go by the kitchen, and Sax isn't surprised to see the door locked shut, red light glowing. In fact, all the other routes seem shut. Even the lights begin to dim as the Oratus walks, until Sax is following a blue familiar through a dark maze, with sole ceiling lights launching spots of brightness. It would be creepy if Sax understood that emotion. Instead, he keeps his claws ready. His mask scanning for hidden anything.

Monsters are scariest in the dark, and there are few monsters worse than Sax.

A green light bursts out of the black, and there's the whooshing sound of a door opening. The familiar turns to Sax and points into a room that has just appeared from a blank section of wall.

"What you're looking for is in here," Dalachite says.

"What I'm looking for? What I'm looking for is you."

"No, no you're not. What you're looking for, what everyone is looking for, are answers. The reason you're here."

Sax slow blinks at the familiar. He's always known why he's here. To eliminate the Sevora. And after them, anything else that poses a threat to the order of the galaxy. There's no other reason. There's no grand mystery.

"You're wrong," Sax says. "I know my purpose."

Laughter comes through the invisible speakers.

"You only think you do. You're part of a grand construct. A game that's been played since before your pathetic race was made."

Sax will enjoy devouring this one.

Again the familiar gestures. Sax goes into the room. He's curious. He doesn't care what Dalachite says, but if there's a threat in here, Sax prefers to neutralize it. If there's not, he's got the weapons to break his way out.

Nonetheless, as he goes by, Sax turns, and with his midclaws, splits the familiar and shreds it to pieces. It'll reform, but the move brings some satisfaction.

As soon as Sax is inside, the door slams shut behind him and lights spring up. Spotlights glow around the ceiling's edges, focusing on the center of the room. The space is large, square, and the middle floor is a series of metal grates, with dozens of small holes. On top of those sits a platform, rising a meter from the ground. Flat and sleek and silver. On it, being dissembled by a set of four familiars, are two Flaum. From the smell, they're fresh bodies.

"The next thaw," Dalachite says. The familiars take pieces and put them into bags, drain fluid into the holes in the floor using small suction tubes.

"What is this?" Sax says the words aloud and in his mind at the same time. It's clear there's a dissection going on, but why? What secrets could the Flaum, a species that has to have been torn apart over and over and over again for cycles, still hold?

"Do you see this?" Dalachite says. "This is what science is. Continual learning. Reaching forth and finding new discoveries. Perfecting those discoveries that we have already made. You see my blue familiars, yes?"

Sax feels an itchy anger. A growing desire to take apart the things in front of his eyes. The horrendous show that he's watching is terrifying, wrong. What is happening on this station?

"Every piece of these Flaum has been preserved. Every part of them will go to my algorithms. Will live on through my familiars."

"Live on?"

"Do you ever wonder, Sax, how I make these familiars?"

Sax doesn't answer. He knows Dalachite's going to explain anyway, and it does.

"I take the cells of the living, spin them and turn them into what you see before you. Yet, they are imperfect. Still so much work to do. So keep going, Sax. Keep going and you'll see."

A door opens on the far side of the room. Beyond the platform. Dalachite means for Sax to keep going. His claws twitch; they want to tear. But Sax resists. As Bas would say, this is about the mission, not the moment.

Sax walks on, around the display and out of the room to the next one. Which is exactly like the first, except a single crucial difference: This platform is on solid, hole-less ground, surrounded by medical machines holding bags and tanks and containers full of what, Sax doesn't know. All of them are pressing, poking, prodding a shape in the middle. One that is the familiar's blue, but also yellow and red in spots. As though true flesh is growing over the fragile familiar goop.

"Everything must grow, Sax. Everything must evolve on itself. It took so long to make the familiars. To get them to the point where they could replace my staff and my robots in the simplest of duties." Dalachite continues on.

Sax can smell a wide range of chemicals. Alcohols, glues, stinging scents of life. The strange ozone iron smell of blood. He takes a step closer to the center platform. Yes, that is hair. It's sprouting from a couple patches on the familiar. Patches that are brownish-blue. Patches that look almost like skin.

"There are always initial imperfections. First models. The ones you see everywhere, demonstrating my concept. Setting expectations for what comes next."

A green light blinks on and another door shunts open. Further.

Sax goes. He's aware this is a show. He's aware of what's going on here, that this isn't for Dalachite's benefit, but for visitors to the station. To those who are invested in its progress. Why else would the Amigga bother with this?

The third room holds something different entirely. It's thin and long. The wall to his right is one large screen. One that immediately lights up and begins to play a short sequence. Creatures slide onto the screen, each occupying their own space.

Sax recognizes the Flaum, the Whelk and the Teven—the strange, pole-dwelling creatures. All of them have green circles around their images. There are others, all with red X's. But there are two missing entirely. His own, the Oratus, and the new ones. The humans.

"As you can see, I have a long way to go. The project is incomplete. In many ways."

At the far end, another way opens. Sax keeps moving. He can't stop now. He's curious in spite of himself. He's angry in spite of his curiosity. The next room holds another platform, but this one is empty. The spotlights angle towards the silver center, leaving the sides of the room in shadow.

"Come, Sax. Won't you help me? Won't you be my next great experiment?" There's a sudden catch over the speakers, a frustrated sigh. "Unfortunately, you're not the only troublemaker on this station. Do enjoy yourself, Sax. I'll be back soon."

This has gone far enough. Sax takes a step towards the center of the room, scans for the doorway, and his mask pings a warning. The bright lights are blinding, they keep Sax from seeing into the dark sides around him. So Sax has the mask switch to infrared viewing.

They're everywhere.

At least a dozen, maybe more. Hugging the walls and now walking towards him. Familiars. Sax can't make out the details from the blobs of orange and reds he's seeing, so he backs up. His tail hits the platform, and Sax climbs on it as his claws draw the pair of black bars from the mask.

With a squeeze, each bar jets out a meter-long blade, nano-sharpened to shear through the thickest armor. The familiars continue to close, and Sax waits. Once they step close, he'll be able to cut them all down.

And they do. A crashing wave coming at Sax from all angles. He begins to cut, to whirl and slash. Green and red fills his vision, and he feels their hands, pulling, beating, tugging.

An endless avalanche.

35 / ESCAPE PLAN

The three of us leave my room in a line. We head towards the two familiars standing guard. They look at us, and I expect Dalachite to ask what we're doing, but no comment comes. Viera leans on me, and instead of going right to the familiars, I suddenly veer left into her room.

There, I do what I did in mine and open the compartment above her bed. Just like in my room, a mask is there. I help her put it on and then we go to Malo's and do the same. They ditch their ratty old clothes from a world that no longer seems quite so real. One of jungles and daylight and desert and rain. Now we're in this one. Home of metal and bright lights.

Our new outfits—the masks cling to our skin like silver, seemingly as we command—elicit no reaction from the familiars. Viera, still leaning on me even with the mask, speaks first. "Left something of mine in the med bay. I'd like to go get it."

"You left nothing in the med bay," Dalachite's voice says. "Now please, I'm busy with something else. Return to your quarters."

My eyes drift to Malo, and he takes charge. We don't have any weapons, but then, neither do the familiars. They stand equal our height, and their bodies are strangely similar to ours. That doesn't mean they know how to fight. That doesn't mean they're human.

Malo jabs the familiar nearest him in the stomach and then, using the momentum of the swing, curls into a backhanded elbow into the familiar on the right. Both stumble back. Both appear, otherwise, entirely fine. They straighten, and again bar the path forward.

"I don't want to hurt you, but you have no right to leave your rooms. You are my subjects. You will stay until I call for you." Dalachite's voice is hard.

"I think we'd rather leave," I say.

You have to rush them together. Push through.

In Charre, I say what Ignos suggests. We charge right for the center, between the two familiars. Malo leading the way, Viera second, with me last. I'm guessing Dalachite won't want to hurt me. That it'll be restrained, slower, with me than the others. Malo angles forward and lowers his shoulder as the familiars move to cross their arms.

Malo's a strong lion warrior of the Charre. He does not bend. He does not give. He pushes and shoves and he cries out for his god. I push Viera behind him and the Lunare stumbles, reaches down and uses her hands to push herself back up from the floor, and so when Malo hits those crossed arms and breaks the familiars to the side of the hallway, we're right behind. Ready to rush through.

I feel blue hands grab at my back. They miss.

We're running. Viera and I follow Malo, and I'm working to keep Viera on her feet. Her breathing is shallow, labored. I see sweat break out underneath her mask, the strange clothing doing what it can to wick it away. She's even paler than before, when the fever drove her to the brink of death.

"Stay alive Viera. Keep moving." I say.

"Don't worry Empress, I won't fall apart on you. Not completely, anyway." Viera replies.

Doorways shut along our path. As they close themselves off, the lights dim. Until suddenly we can't see anything anymore, except for single train of bright spots leading us forward. We stop, and I turn around, expecting to see the two familiars following, but they're nowhere.

"Since you persist, I will show you what you want to see. Show you where you need to go. Follow the lights, my subjects, and you will find your answers," Dalachite says, its voice booming out around them.

"Do we follow?" Malo says.

"I don't see we have any choice," I say. "But let's be ready. Because I'm guessing this doesn't lead us to the docking bay."

We move forward, Malo still in front, Viera in the middle and me in back. It's a slow walk, and I use the time to pester Ignos with questions. Try to get some idea of what's going on, but its not sure.

The Amigga will try to capture you. That's all I can say.

I could figure that out for myself.

The lights eventually lead us to a sealed door, red light glaring at us. I reach and place a hand on the metal, but it doesn't open. The mask fails to unlock it too, finding no connection.

"We followed the lights." I say to the air.

"You did. You did. If you would please wait just a moment, there are preparations that need taking care of," Dalachite says.

I look at both Viera and Malo. "I don't think this is going to end well."

"Can't give up hope yet, Empress," Viera says. "We're still alive, aren't we?"

"For the moment," I reply.

Malo hammers his hand in the door twice more. "Open it up. Kill us if you're going to, or let us go."

To my surprise, the door does what Malo says. It slides up and open. In the room, which is brightly lit by an array of spotlights, waits a single large gray platform. On the floor beneath it are metal plates punctured with dozens of small holes. It all glistens, as though it's been washed recently.

"Now if you would please proceed, the three of you, onto the platform. We can begin." Dalachite's voice echoes off the walls.

We walk inside and the door shuts behind me. I turn, but the only panel is dead black and unresponsive.

We're trapped.

36 / NEVER STOP

He fights himself into a corner. They keep coming at Sax, even though his blades are whirling, cutting every new arrival into pieces. They keep coming because they know his swings will slow, he'll start to miss, and eventually they'll pull Sax apart. As if that's not enough, Sax notices the familiars getting larger as the ones he cuts absorb into the next wave. It's a futile onslaught getting worse by the second.

Blue hands grasp at Sax's face and arms. They scratch and pull until Sax bites or slashes them away, buying micro-seconds of reprieve before the next familiar fills the gap. There's no way he survives if this keeps up. No way Sax can win an infinite war.

So, in those micro-seconds, Sax searches for a solution.

There are two doors in the room. The way he came in, and another, to his right. With a wall of familiars standing in between either choice. He ducks another couple of punches and retaliates by slicing off the arms that threw them.

The crush continues.

Both doors have red-glowing lights above, and Sax doesn't expect Dalachite will open them. He'll have to use his miners. He has two attached to the mask, around his midclaws. Sax grabs one with his left while doing a wide, clearing sweep with the blades held by his fore-claws to get some space. Prepares to take a leap, and then does so.

Unlike the training room, this one doesn't have a high ceiling, and the shallow angle lets blue hands grab at Sax's legs and tail, and they pull him back into the mob. Sax waves the swords as he gets pulled down. Cuts away his attackers, earns himself a new clearing as he hits the floor. He's surrounded, though, so he can't stay there.

Sax scrambles back towards the platform, the one place where he can get a clear shot.

His legs power him forward, and Sax uses the one midclaw he has free to grab the lip of the platform and pull himself up. Or tries to; more hands grab his tail and yank Sax back the other way. He spins, bringing the swords to bear, but the familiars are ready.

Some get cut while others duck the swings or dance back. Then they dart forward again before Sax can recover, pin his arms. Grab the blades themselves even as the edges slash into their skin. Blue goop spatters everywhere, an ocean of it, but the living slime swims back towards familiars the moment it hits a surface.

Sax stays focused. The door. That's the objective. He angles his miner towards it with his left midclaw and pulls the trigger. The short blast, a white-blue bolt, lances through the familiars and strikes the door, burns a hole into it. Then grasping hands rip the miner away. Three familiars grab it and even Sax's midclaw isn't a match for that much strength. The familiars kick the miner back through the onslaught as they swarm forward.

Sax gnashes his teeth, kicks with his legs, slashes with every free claw he has, but he's being buried and he knows it. A trio of familiars presses Sax to the ground, and he catches sight of his stolen miner, lying on the floor beyond his feet. Too far away to grab, but it gives him an idea.

Sax darts his head forward, taking a bite out of the familiar pinning his right midclaw to the ground, and fills his mouth with blue slime. Uses the moment of freedom to pull the other miner from his mask, angles it down along his own body, and, with blue fingers stuffing his mouth, pressing into his eyes and the vents along his chest, pulls the trigger.

Sax doesn't even see the beam, but he hears the result.

A white, boiling heat washes over him. The mask isn't able to deal with it, and Sax feels the skin of his tail and legs burn as the protective shield melts away. Bright flashes and roiling orange flow through Sax's vision. The infrared goes completely red and white, so Sax blinks back to normal spectrum.

Turns out shooting one miner into the battery of another makes a miniature apocalypse.

The lights are gone, and instead all Sax can see are streaks of scattered flame clinging to the walls, to the floor and ceiling. The blast scattered familiar remnants everywhere, the goop turning into bubbling black with the heat. Dark smoke and charred smells fill the room.

Sax stays low, forces his legs, which screech at him with pain, to move. He scrambles over the flames, towards the door he shot open. There's no familiars left. Or if there are, they haven't reformed, and with the flames devouring every trace of leftover goop, Sax doesn't think they're coming back.

Sax throws himself at the door, which doesn't present an obstacle; it just falls away, weakened by the miner shot and the subsequent explosion. The hallway is cool, clear, brightly lit. There are no doors off of this one. Just a long corridor heading, Sax knows, towards the station center. Towards where Dalachite lives.

The Oratus slumps against a side, the cold white bulkhead serving as support. Takes a breath. Then another and a third as smoke wafts out overhead.

This one is going to hurt. Most of Sax's tail is numb, his legs too. A look along his body shows his gray scales turning black. He'll need a long time in the healing tanks.

But that's for later. Now there's the mission. Dalachite still lives.

Sax pulls himself to his feet. It hurts, but the muscles still respond. Badly burned, yes, but not severed. Not melted into nothing.

Fury pushes the Oratus forward.

37 / THE STUFF OF LIFE

The door barely closes before there's a loud bang somewhere nearby. The three of us stare at each other, and Dalachite, which had been finishing its command for us to walk to the center platform, cuts off abruptly. Leaves us in silence.

"What do you suppose that was?" Viera says.

I don't know, but I don't say that, I just stare at Malo, who's looking at the far door.

"I think it's the other ones. The creatures who brought us here," Malo says. "The one, Sax? He doesn't like this place. He doesn't trust those blue things."

"If he's trying to destroy this station, then I'd rather us not be on it," Viera says and I agree.

Which means we have to find a way out. The door we came through is still unresponsive. Same thing with the other exit. We walked in here, and now we're stuck.

"Dalachite wants us to get on the platform," Malo says. "Maybe we should?"

"Following its orders already got us here," I say. "Following them again would just make things worse."

"No, no," Dalachite's voice bursts into the room. "It will not make them worse. No worse than they already are. Rather, it will give you purpose." His words have heat in them now. Anger, rage even. "You'll get on the platform, and you'll lay there and you'll wait. You'll wait because that is what subjects do. That is your job."

We look at each other. "I'm not going to," I say.

Careful Kaishi. This is not one creature you want to anger.

"What the Empress commands, I do," Malo says.

"This isn't an ask. It's not a request. It's an order," Dalachite says. "One I'm willing to enforce."

The far door, not the one we came in, shunts open. Standing there are a pair of hideous creatures. They are brown and patchy, and where the fur is not, there are blue streaks. The same smooth skin of the other familiars. Their eyes are blank and black, and wisps of hair fall from them onto the floor.

They're unstable. Strange.

"What are—" Viera doesn't finish the sentence before the two of them grab Malo and haul him to the platform.

Viera is too hurt to react, but I step forward, snatch at one of their arms and try to pull, but it doesn't move. I've felt the other familiars. The blue ones. They're strong, but not mountains. I had a chance to resist their strength, but these, it's like trying to pull a stone. As though the flimsy blue has been buttressed by taut muscle.

"Do not struggle, subjects." Dalachite's words are followed by Malo hitting the silver platform.

As he does so, one familiar reaches underneath and pulls out a long silver rod. I'm trying a kick and the familiar takes the blow without a care, then turns and pushes me away onto the ground.

It places the rod over Malo's struggling legs, and the rod snaps. Flexes itself around Malo's thighs and squeezes tight. The other familiar places a second rod around Malo's chest, trapping his arms to his sides.

Viera and I look at the odds as the two monsters turn towards us. There's no question of us fighting them. Not with Viera was weak as she is, not with me unarmed. Dalachite calls for us to surrender, and we do so.

The familiars direct us onto the platform with Malo, order us to lie against each other in a row of three.

"Now I'm sorry you had to witness my experiments," Dalachite says. "They're not quite ready yet, as you can see. However, some unexpected difficulties are forcing me to use extra measures."

Wait for an opportunity, Kaishi. The Amigga is distracted. We'll have a chance.

I understand what Ignos is saying, and the familiars haven't wrapped us in metal bars like they did Malo. Instead, when the familiars reach beneath the platform, they bring up clear, rippled tubes that slink down into the holes in the floor. Each one has, on the end, a long, sharp needle. It's not hard to guess what they're going to do with those.

"I didn't think you would hurt us," I protest. "We're your subjects. Your prize experiments."

"Oh you are," Dalachite replies. "The most interesting subjects I've studied since the start of this station. Perhaps in my entire existence. However, I must put *Cobalt* ahead of any single test, any single specimen. That means you three will be worth more to me dead than alive."

"You'll never learn everything about us," I'm saying it frantically,

I've no idea if it's true. No idea what the Amigga is capable of.

"Little one, you must remember, I have your shuttle. I have its records. I can simply send someone to gather more of you. Bring back as many humans as I want. Now, do close your eyes. It will be easier that way."

The familiar gets close. I'm clearly the first choice, as one of the brown patchy nightmares lines up at my head and another at my feet.

Viera tenses, and I feel like she's about to pounce.

"Don't," I say. I speak in Malo's language, and hope Dalachite still can't understand. "Wait for my move, then you go."

Viera nods slightly.

The familiars, tubes in each hand, bring the points towards me. The needles glisten in the bright light. Stabbing straight for my legs, my arms. Centimeters away when I move.

In the jungle, playing games as a child, we rolled around. Somersaulted underneath knotted vines and low branches. Played tricks and tags on each other. So it's second nature for me to kick my legs up, bring them to my chest, though I feel the slight scratch as a needles catch the bare ends of my feet. I keep rolling back and press my hands on the side of the platform. Feel the needles of the familiar behind me scratch my shoulders, but I ignore the sting. The mask blunts some of it anyway.

I press off.

I don't so much hit, as fall into the familiar standing behind my head. It drops the tubes as we both fall back, and I strike it high enough that it overbalances and collapses to the ground. The other one is rushing around the platform when Viera kicks out her left foot, hits the familiar in the leg and trips the thing. It falls hard, and then Viera, lacking mobility, rolls off the platform on top of it. Lands on the familiar and starts punching.

I slip off of mine, grab the tubes from the floor, and try to avoid glancing at the red wet on the needle points. My familiar starts to get back up and as it does so, as it turns its brown patchy blue face towards me, I jam the needles into it.

Deep.

The tubes start to shake as the needles dig all the way in, and I realize I've kicked off some mechanism. The familiar lurches back, but I've put the tubes in far enough that I see little metal wires spring out from the tops of them. The wires grip into the familiar's skin, holding the needles steady and then I watch as the stuff that makes the familiar begins to drain through the tubes, filling them with blue slime. The familiar begins to shrink down before me as the tubes drain its very life away.

That's what would've happened to me. My blood, my muscles, skin and bones, all of it sucked away into *Cobalt*'s bowels.

"This is very unexpected," Dalachite's voice comes over as Viera continues to struggle with her familiar. "All of my experiments are going rather wrong today."

I ignore the thing. Scrabble across the floor to where Viera's fighting. Towards were Viera's getting thrown off her opponent and slammed against the wall. Towards where Viera's crumpling in a heap. This familiar doesn't have its tubes anymore—it dropped them on the far side of the platform—so I've nothing to stab it with, nothing to grapple with, except my own hands.

Which prove ineffective.

The familiar doesn't hesitate. It grabs me, crushes me tight in its arms and holds me to its chest, and then I feel it run. We dash towards the far door that it came in, which opens as it nears, and then shuts behind us.

As it closes, I hear Malo shout my name.

And then there's nothing else.

38 / FAMILIAR FRAME

Sax lurches down the hallway. Slow. He doesn't remember this from the map. No idea where he's going, but there seems to be only one way, so that's where he heads. All Sax knows is that *Cobalt* is a long, triangular extension from a sphere in the middle. As long as he's heading towards the center, he'll get where he wants to be eventually.

The hallway ends in a rounded door with a glowing red light, as per usual. Sax raises his claws, the only weapons he has left.

"Don't," Dalachite says. "You've damaged quite enough of my station already. If you want through, I'll open this."

Sax doesn't care to reply. He doesn't have the energy, the focus to taunt. He gives the creature a moment, holding the miner towards the door, when the light flashes green and it opens. On the other side is what's called a band room. A chamber that circles the center of a station without walls in between. Rare to have, and costly, but if you need the space, this is the way to do it.

Dalachite is putting that space to good use: stretching out in front of Sax in either direction is a long chain. Large plastic bars move, pulled by what Sax guesses are programmed magnets, in a slow loop across the wide, flat silver surface. Each bar spans the width of the room, and Sax can see their tops are grated with fine steel. The bar bottoms are coated with small nozzles. Nozzles that, as the bars move, squeeze out the same blue stuff that makes up the familiars. They're layering the slime on the silver floor, which is divided into long thin sections going perpendicular to the plastic bars.

Sax realizes what this is, what's going on.

The layering bars create familiars. A couple dozen at a time or more. The dripping goop builds them into beings. Sax doesn't even have the energy to move. To act. He simply watches, mesmerized, as the bars go around and around and around and then the wave is done. The whole line pauses for just a second, the bars sliding up to the ceiling, which parts and allows a new batch of goop to refill the bars.

There's a soft buzzing sound and a slight stinging smell fills the room. Current; strong electricity. Evidenced further by the twitching familiar forms. After the sound dies, each one sits up, slowly. Then stands, rising off the silver platform. They all turn and look at Sax.

"There you have it," Dalachite says. "The source of my servants. Nothing so brilliant to one who's seen the galaxy, I'm sure."

Except Sax hasn't ever seen anything like this, and he knows why: if this can be everywhere, anywhere, then what need would anyone have of other species? The Amigga, *this* Amigga, could run whole worlds with these things.

Sax asks the one question still burning in his mind, "How do you control them?"

"Simple, really," Dalachite says. "Consider the Sevora. Consider how it places its own commands into a target's nerves. How it supersedes the host and sends its messages throughout. All I've done is take a bit of Sevora into my own self. All I've done is splice my own genetic material into all of these. They are my familiars, after all."

"Sevora can't communicate through air," Sax hisses back. "They need to be inside you. They have to capture you."

"Do they? If the Sevora ever truly looked at themselves, they would know that everything they do is biological impulse. That everything they share with their hosts comes via signals. Specific frequencies, specific micro-volts. It's not hard to send those same signals throughout the station. It's not hard to convince a staff of willing followers to set up a mechanism for you to do this, especially when they don't realize it's going to be their own end to do so."

"Then you are no better than the parasites we're fighting," Sax says.

"I don't believe I ever claimed to be. The real fault of the Sevora, of course, is that they failed to establish their power before we realized they were there. I won't make that mistake. The Amigga won't make that mistake."

"You already have."

He may be burned, he might be exhausted, but Sax still has four clawed arms and a mouth full of teeth. He sets about using them.

These familiars barely know what they're doing; their movements are slow and jerky. Sax tears through them like grass. Shreds them to pieces and then makes sure to grab the bars as well, gouging up the room's wall to the great metal things. His claws take time to cut through the thick bars, but Sax slashes every one of them in two. It's hard, moving around the band, but at its center, *Cobalt* is a much smaller station than at the outskirts.

Every bang of the bar pieces hitting the floor is a victory.

"Now I want to see you make your army." Sax glares around the room, unsure of where the cameras are.

"First I welcomed you to *Cobalt*. Then you tricked me, lied and sought to destroy my creations. Now, again, you rip apart what you don't even know. You, Oratus, are the single greatest example of our failure." Dalachite is howling now. "Because of you, my own progress is set back cycles. Do you know how long it will take to repair this? To bring back those familiars that you burned?"

"I don't care." Sax is hunting for the next door to the station's core, but there doesn't seem to be one.

"You don't care? How like an Oratus. How like you to disregard all science just so you can pursue your tearing of flesh and drinking of blood—"

Dalachite continues to rage, but Sax tunes it out. There must be a way from here deeper into the station. The Amigga has to feed. It can't seal itself off entirely. Sax clomps across the silver printing floor to the far end. Scans the wall. Flips the mask to infrared, and there. He sees it. Behind one section, a different color. Lower air pressure, cooler temps. Sax moves over to it, stares at the plate. Now that he's here, he can pick out the lines. A disguised sliding door, but why?

Dalachite falls silent. It must realize what Sax is looking at. "Do you know what Oratus? Do you know what you have forgotten in your quest to destroy me?"

"Do tell," Sax says. He takes his claws and jabs them into the wall, points first. The metal resists, but not for long. It's too thin, not made to withstand an Oratus strike. Sax breaks through and begins to tear it asunder.

"You forgot that you're not alone on this station. You've forgotten your pair. Your humans."

Sax keeps ripping and tearing. Bas can take care of herself. The humans, though, aren't as capable, and if Bas is guarding the shuttle, then no one is helping them.

"I will do whatever is necessary to keep you away from me, Oratus. Even if it means destroying my most prized subjects."

"Do you have them?" Sax asks.

"They are screaming beneath my knives even now," Dalachite says. "But, if you agree to let me live, if you agree to leave the station, I'll let you have them. I will let you all go."

The metal door falls away, the shreds of it revealing an older, darker hallway leading farther. Sax sees other entrances off to the sides. Storerooms, most likely. The food and drink Dalachite needs to survive.

Except, the humans.

Sax is so close now, but if he kills Dalachite, or if he tries and the humans die, then it's as Bas says, the mission fails. Their chance at peace fails.

"Do we have a deal, Oratus?"

39 / SPARK OF RESISTANCE

It's dark in the room. For a moment. Then, as the familiar drags me along with one arm, the entire wall to my right lights up in white. Strange shapes begin to populate the space. The first one is brown, furry. Like the familiar dragging me, only without the blue patches. Next to it appears a strange slug-like creature, and a third, long and straight, with what seems like a shell covering its body and little arms and eyes popping out of holes. Several more appear, one rounded with what looks like many small feet jutting from its central circle.

This one, unlike the first three, is shaded red.

I'm looking at them because I can't think of anything else. I'm breathing fast, my heart thundering as the familiar pulls me along the floor. I'm panicking, even though I've been in life or death situations before, and I know why: the sacrifice at the top of the Vaos, the fight with the Lunare, I understood where I was and what was happening. Here, nothing makes sense. The familiar has no place in my society, in my knowledge of the universe.

It does now.

Ignos isn't helping.

We're halfway along when a thunk echoes behind us. A

pounding on the door. Viera, unless Malo found a way to free himself from those metal bars. Either way, the noise makes the familiar glance back. Over my head and away.

Fight back.

I do it almost without thinking. I catch Ignos' suggestion, its attempted command of my muscles, which goes nowhere but into my mind. I plant my left foot and throw my shoulder into a falling twist. It's a heavy move, but the familiar is a heavy creature. Stronger than me, but it's not expecting my attempt. Its feet slip as I swing my body and its grip falls loose as it curls around. The momentum sends the familiar right into the great white display, which it hits, and the screen shatters. The entire thing flickers and dies as the familiar, body still sticking out towards me, twitches while sparks fly around it.

I stand up slow, stare at it. Wait for the familiar to get back up and come after me, but it doesn't.

Don't wait. Go.

So I do. I run back to the closed door we came through, but the light is red and I don't see a way to open it. The mask doesn't help me either. I look back at the familiar, but it's still stuck there. Not moving anymore.

There'll be others. Is there another way out?

There is. At the end of the hallway, visible in the screen's sputtering light. An open door, though I can only see shadows through it. Still, with nowhere else to go, I head that way. Run down the hall, past the familiar's body, and into another room. There are no lights here, and the white that I see is coming from what looks like a broken door at the other end.

Mounds of blackened liquid sit throughout; curled and burned onto the floors and ceilings. Some of the piles glow orange in parts, radiating heat. The room smells of smoke and char. It's a place of death, and I don't stay there.

I move into a long hallway, and stop on the other side of the door. At the other end is the creature that took me, the Oratus. It's standing large, though I notice there appear to be black burns all over the lower half of its body. Sax takes a limping step towards me.

"Stop," I say.

Not that I think I can command it to do anything, but it seems hurt. Less deadly than before.

"Where are the other two?" Sax asks me, his voice a hissing rasp.

"Behind me. Locked in another room." I think for a second. "Can you free them?"

"They're safe?"

"For now." I guess I don't know that for sure, but there hadn't been any familiars in the room when I left. Hopefully, it's stayed that way. "But if we can get back there?"

Sax shakes his head. "You are the most important, and the Amigga is the greatest threat. We go back. Now."

The Oratus turns a slow circle and I stare at its long tail. Forearms, those glistening claws. There's a faint glimmer between its lower torso and its upper, and I realize that it's wearing a mask. One that's only half there.

I can't believe I'm saying this, but you should follow it. That Oratus is our best chance of getting out of this alive.

Follow it? It's going away from my friends. I can't leave them.

If you help it take care of the Amigga, your friends will live. It's the only way.

The only way. How often had I heard Ignos say that? Talk about destiny. Plans. The sure route to achieving my hopes and dreams.

"I'm going back for them," I say down the hall as I turn around.

"If you do," says Sax to my back. "I'll die. You'll die. Every one of the people you know on Earth will be taken and used by this creature to make more of those familiars. This is our chance. Do not be a coward."

I look at my hands. They are still a girl's hands. Weathered by jungle years, yes, but otherwise young. I don't have many battle scars. I don't have decades of courage building me up to this moment. How am I supposed to help a deadly creature like Sax fight Dalachite?

Not everything is won with strength. Sometimes, just an open eye and a willingness to take advantage is enough.

Then I hear something I don't expect. A low rasp, as if the Oratus can't quite believe he's saying it either.

"Please."

You must, Kaishi. Help him.

I flash back to the sessions, stuck on that platform while strange images flare in front of my eyes. Feeling Ignos crawl in and out of my head as Dalachite and its familiars force the Sevora to move. The sheer panic moments ago when a nightmare thing drags me away.

"If we are going to kill this thing, let's do it fast." I meet Sax's eyes, let him know I'm not scared. "I want to save my friends."

40 / TOGETHER

The human girl is courageous. Sax is happier than he would've thought to see that. He won't be going into the Amigga's chamber alone. The last encounter with the mature Sevora on the seed ship floats fresh in his memory. How easily things could be turned against a single person. How crucial a partner.

Sax wishes it could be Bas here instead of this little human, but he'll work with what he can get. They head back to the ruined familiar factory, and when Kaishi asks Sax what happens here, he tells her.

"This is where the familiars are made."

"Were made, I think."

Sax waves his foreclaws at the destruction. "This is what *I* was made for."

The two of them cross the floor. Head towards the next door. Metal shards litter the entryway.

"I thought we had a deal, Oratus," Dalachite's voice booms out of somewhere.

"The deal required the humans to be captured," Sax replies. "As you can see, they are not."

"One, perhaps. But the other two—"

"Will survive," Kaishi says. "They're warriors and they know what they're fighting for."

"And just what is that?" the Amigga counters.

"Humanity," Kaishi replies.

Sax isn't waiting anymore. He goes through the door, Kaishi behind him. There are two sealed doors on the sides of the next hallway, and one circular, large one at the end. Dim light makes it harder to see than before.

As they pass by, the first door shoots open. No light locks on these. Perhaps there's no need, this deep in *Cobalt*. Regardless, it's easy to see what's inside. Boxes of stored supplies. Apparently lifted back in here right off the ships. Nothing that concerns Sax and the human, so they go on to the end. The other door, on the right, remains closed. Sax almost checks it, almost tries to see if it opens, but they're so close now. Too close to waste time on distractions.

Sax turns to Kaishi as they stand outside the door. "When it opens, I don't know what we'll find on the other side. Stay composed. Stay ready to move. I'll draw its attention, and you find ways to help where you can."

Sax knows the mask is only covering his upper body. His head. There's plenty of pain from his legs, but he's got enough left to do this. Enough left to brave the Amigga. The door isn't locked: at a touch from Sax's claw on its surface, it shunts open. There, in front of them, is a vast room twice the size of the seed ship's center. Catwalks ring the chamber, extending from the door and looping around the middle. The walkway in front of them extends to a platform in the center. On it rests the Amigga. Part of it, anyway. Dalachite itself extends from its core to the edges of the chamber. It looks less like a living creature and more like a synapse. A central cluster of organs and tissue with numerous branches spitting out towards the sides, to ports and terminals where they've immersed themselves.

The lighting is intense and multicolored. Glowing from hundreds of terminals showing all manner of different data. All of them connected with hard Amigga fiber to the creature's main core. *Cobalt* is part of the Amigga, and the Amigga part of the station. Destroy one, and Sax would likely destroy the other, at least in any functional sense.

"So you made it here. Congratulations." Dalachite sighs. "You've ruined my experiments. Destroyed my familiars. Rendered all the progress I've made over so much time meaningless. Are you happy, Oratus? Are you happy you've defied your masters?"

"No," Sax replies. He's noticed Kaishi staring open-mouthed at what she's seeing. He needs to buy time for her to get composed, to be ready when the fight breaks out. "Defying orders doesn't make me happy, but using these claws to rend you and your creations to pieces will."

Sax takes a step forward. He's promised to draw fire, and that's what he'll do. He scans the room for weapons, hoping the mask will pick out any that he can't see first. But there's none. As though Dalachite, living on a research station, never considered that one day it might be attacked.

"Do you know who your commanders really are?" Dalachite says, and it's disconcerting to Sax to see the creature talking to them, but hear the voice come from all over.

The Amigga has no mouth. All the other Amigga that Sax has seen, without their own stations, use mobile suits. Mechanical accessories and prosthetics to make their way around. Those have clear speakers. Those offer clear targets.

"I know who they are." Sax is content to let Dalachite talk, and stops his advance.

Sax uses the seconds to plan a strategy. The first goal is simple—sever as many connections as possible. Make it so Dalachite can't access *Cobalt*'s systems. So that, at the least, the Amigga can't set *Cobalt* to self-destruct while they're on it.

"We are your commanders, Oratus. The Amigga. We created you, we own you. And you shall obey."

As Dalachite says this, there's a shunting rumble throughout the station. Sax hears a whine behind him, and he whirls in time to see a Flaum, an old chocolate-colored one coming into the room behind Kaishi, with white fringes on his fur, holding a miner.

The Flaum fires.

The blast catches Sax in the stomach. There's no impact from a laser, no force, but the burning, searing bolt set Sax's nerves aflame and he stumbles back along the catwalk and then off of it. He bounces down and hits a pair of the Amigga's thick, trunk-like connections, before rolling to a resting place at the very bottom of the sphere.

41 / THE CARETAKER

I see Sax fall. Turn and look at where the blast came from. The creature is about my size. Fur the color of mud with ashen fringes, and weathered, bat-like face. It's wearing a loose uniform with faded colors; greens and browns. It levels the stubby, thick weapon at me, but doesn't pull the trigger.

"Now Kaishi," Dalachite says, its voice coming from speakers around the sphere, so that it seems to echo from everywhere. "You know I don't want to hurt you. You know you have so much promise. Yes, yes this foul Oratus damaged me. Set us back. But you and I, we can rebuild the station. You can join Coorvin here and make it whole again. Set the universe on its rightful path."

I don't hold much with what Dalachite says. It's already tried to kill me multiple times, and the monster itself looks so crazy and terrifying that I'm having a hard time putting together coherent thoughts.

Ignos, though, helps me.

What you're looking at is the Amigga's caretaker. Every Amigga has to have one, once it gets settled. After all, look at it. It can't move. It can't even feed itself.

Coorvin, which I gather is the furry thing's name, stares at my face. I see glimmers of intelligence in those beady black eyes, but the mouth doesn't move. It shot Sax, so I can't regard it as a friend, but then, attacking it might mean I wind up the same as the Oratus—charred at the bottom of the chamber. So I hesitate. Decide to fall back on what I do best: ask questions.

"What should I do?" I say aloud, ask it of Dalachite, of Coorvin, and Ignos.

Coorvin replies first, in a hoarse, light rasp. "Help me."

"Yes, help him," Dalachite says. "Say the word, Kaishi. We can even spare those other specimens. Your friends. You'll all be together here on *Cobalt*. You'll all work with me. You'll never want or need for anything ever again."

I'm not picking up that vibe from Coorvin. That all his cares are gone and he's living a blissful life onboard *Cobalt*. There's pain in his tight face. Like he's struggling with something. So I take a step towards him.

Kaishi, what are you doing? Don't antagonize–

I push Ignos away. The Sevora isn't human. The Sevora hasn't seen this look before. But I have. I saw it in the eyes of the sacrifice on the top of the Vaos in Damantum. I saw in Viera's eyes before she passed out as I cauterized her wounds. The look of someone waiting to be rescued, of someone needing another's help.

I can't resist that.

"What is he?" I ask the Amigga. "Coorvin?"

"Oh, he's a Flaum. My caretaker. Implanted, of course, to make sure I can influence him as necessary. I need him less with my familiars, but I've made sure he's lived a long and fruitful life. And I may need him yet, until I'm certain the familiars can handle every duty without issue."

I move closer to Coorvin, and he turns his weapon towards me, that wide black barrel aiming squarely at my chest. Ignos screams at me, telling me to say something, to do something.

So I step quick. Past the point of the weapon. Coorvin starts to twist, but he's slow. I lay my hands on the barrel, grab it. The weapon's still warm from the shot fired at Sax. Coorvin tries to move it away from me, but I'm stronger than he is. Stronger than an old Flaum. It's not hard to pull the weapon from his hands.

"Kaishi, what are you doing?" Dalachite says. "You must understand, hurting me will not help you. You'll still be stuck on the station. Be a prisoner here forever. Without me, you'll never leave. You'll doom Coorvin too—he'll never get more food. Another chance to go home."

I swing the weapon around, point it at the Amigga. "You weren't going to let us go home anyway."

Dalachite quivers, ripples moving up and down its skin and the connections to the walls. Strange purple lines illuminate up and down the thing's body, and a wet sheen drips out from those lines to coat the creature.

"You could just come close, Kaishi. End your struggle now. Find peace. I'm not above mercy for my subjects."

The Flaum, behind me, makes a move. Tackles me. Coorvin isn't heavy, but he's enough to throw me off balance. I hit the laced metal floor and the weapon bounces from my hands, rolls off the edge of the catwalk.

As Coorvin grabs for me, I kick him away, my foot connecting with his face. Coorvin staggers back, puts his furry hands up to his head, closes his eyes and shakes back and forth. I climb to my feet.

Hear Dalachite's laughter.

"Now you've lost your weapon, Kaishi. What are you going to do, beat on me with those fists of yours? I'd like to see you try. That is the one thing I would've changed about your kind. But they didn't ask me. No, no they did not."

I don't know what he's talking about, and Ignos feels just as confused. Still, I have to find some way of destroying this thing. Then I remember. I glance behind me, the door to leave the chamber is still open. I back through.

"Running away? Or have you decided that you truly belong on the station?" I hear Dalachite ask as I go.

I don't reply.

Inside the hallway, I see the second door, one that didn't open when we first came through, has slid aside to reveal spare accommodations. Where Coorvin had been hiding. In the room to the right, the supplies still sit. Crates bearing names and terms that I don't recognize. No weapons, no solutions here.

I head back to the broad chamber where Sax claimed the familiars were made. It's not far, and there, split into pieces, are the metal bars with the nozzles. The things Sax said created the familiars. I take a piece. It's taller and longer than me, but I'm able to lift it. Either I've become stronger since coming here, or there's something else going on.

I run back down the hallway, carrying it before me.

No, Kaishi. Don't.

No time for new plans. I use the metal bar like a spear. Dive right into Dalachite's chamber, keep my feet pounding on. Coorvin recognizes what I'm about to do—I see his furry head jerk, his paws reach towards me, but he's a second too slow. I thrust the metal head right into the glistening, mottled Amigga skin. The spear bites into Dalachite, and I hear it scream.

A scream that changes, quick, to a gurgling laugh. I try to pull back on the spear, but it's stuck. Before I can react, the Amigga twists its body, rotating itself and the spear, with my hands around it, so that I'm lifted into the air above the creature. I notice, then, that the spear is smoking, melting down into the Amigga.

Its skin is coated in absorbent acid. It's how they eat, Kaishi.

"Clever, so clever you've killed your self," Dalachite chuckles through the speakers. "The Amigga would never make a species smarter than us. Always with weaknesses. Always with flaws we can exploit."

Make a species?

I try to climb to the top of my makeshift spear. Feel the jagged edges cut into my hands as I grip my way up. The bar creaks as the Amigga continues to melt it away. I risk a glance down; it's only a meter now to that glistening, burning ball of flesh. The remnants of the spear, as they disintegrate, spread out beneath me in a pale yellow spot.

"But at least it worked. At least they succeeded," Dalachite continues to talk. "Do you know how long we tried? How many species failed us?"

Another moment, another half-meter closer. I think if I time it right, as soon as I hit the Dalachite's skin, I can jump. The mask should protect me that long. I hope. I adjust, widen my stance as I hold onto the top of the spear. Get ready.

"It's been a long time since I've had fresh meat. A milestone, as well. I imagine it's the first time any Amigga has tried human." Dalachite says as the tips of my toes dangle just above its shimmering skin.

There's a bright flash. Blue and white, iridescent. It burns and boils up through the Amigga. Turning the brown and green skin of the creature black and orange as it fries and bursts its body into flame.

My spear creaks and breaks at the heat, and I plunge into the boiling inferno.

42 / LAST ACTS

Sax is dying.

There's a hole burned into, through his chest. A miner at close range and a damaged mask is a mortal equation. That he's fading out of existence, the left of his two hearts torched to nothing, isn't what bothers the Oratus.

It's the thought of a mission unfinished. A goal left standing.

Which is why the clatter of the miner as it slides down the sphere towards him sparks dim, blurred life in Sax's nerves. His eyes break through the veil of pain and he sees it, black and dented and scraped but there. Within reach of his right midclaw. The only noise he hears is a ringing, aching echo. The only smell the spicy char of his own scales.

His midclaw moves in a jerk. Sharp, short. Sax's energy comes like that now. Spasms. But it's enough for the razor points to find their grip. The miner is made for Flaum, though, which means Sax doesn't have points for his claws. The trigger is shaped for a finger—rounded and large. With another yank, Sax pulls the weapon close to him. The metal is cold. So cold that it takes Sax a second to realize it's not, in fact, the metal he's feeling but the icy chill of his body shutting down. His legs are lost to him. He can't move his tail. It's like a lit room gone suddenly dark—Sax has no grasp of things he once knew so well.

But he has a grasp of one thing. Sax moves his right foreclaw, wraps it around the close part of the barrel, then, with both claws, swings the weapon up so that the butt of it rests against Sax's chest. This brings with it a rippling sensation as the miner bends and bursts his blistered scales. There's a spike of pain, and Sax can feel himself wanting to pass out.

To slip away.

He returns to a memory, his first formal training, when Sax is standing in a line. There are five other Oratus, four to his left, one, Bas, to his right. They stand on a long, flat plain on a planet whose name, now, blurs to nothing. It's all rock and dust anyway, a place long abandoned by any life of note and now used, thanks to its breathable atmosphere, as an Oratus base. Their school. Their home.

Along either side of the tanned, rocky plain are set tall, black pillars. Nubs extend from some, acting as hubs to smaller pillar spokes. Twenty in all, and they hum with the audible pulse of power. Their teacher, an Oratus with blue-green scales, raises a foreclaw, then drops it. As he does so, Sax, Bas and the others, break into long, loping strides. Until they pass the first pillar. It's a cacophonous, destructive sound. Ringing pulses that make Sax's nerves vibrate like a ringing bell. He keeps moving, because there is no alternative. There is no choice for an Oratus. No other way.

The next pillar launches stinging bolts of electricity, ones that strike him with numbing force. Then there is fire, cold, noxious gasses and worse as they pass through the Thrashing Wheels. Together, the Oratus struggle through. They push their way to the end. And when they get there, helping each other to stand, the blue-green instructor is waiting, and he points back the way they've come.

Again.

And again.

And again.

Sax steadies the miner with his left foreclaw—his left midclaw, too close to the miner's blast, has, like his legs and tail, vanished from his consciousness. He rests his head back on the metal floor. It's not hard to make out what's above him: the latticed catwalk, and through it, the brown bulk of the Amigga. There's motion too, sliding through the grease-blur of his eyes; what looks like silver, stabbing forward towards Dalachite.

The human. Kaishi.

The species has more courage than Sax expects. More than their weak, squishy bodies suggest. But she doesn't know that you don't fight an Amigga up close. Stay back. Fire away. Now she's caught. Dalachite's taking her weapon, and Kaishi herself.

The development doesn't change Sax's plan. Just means he has to adjust his aim. Doesn't want to hit the human. So he lowers the angle of the miner. Off-center now, but a burn like this ought to be enough. Sax presses down with his right midclaw, pushes and holds the trigger in. There's no kick—a miner runs on energy, and there's no recoil there. The blue-white bolt that comes out, that keeps burning, is beautiful. Grand and spectacular and Sax would watch it for infinity if he could.

The miner melts through the catwalk, hits the bottom-front part of the Amigga. The liquid coating the creature's skin superheats, bursts into its own flame that spreads across the entire creature. Dalachite's connections to *Cobalt* shrivel and blacken, burning skin falling around Sax like volcanic rain.

Sax realizes he's still holding the trigger and lets go. The world seems dark for an instant when the bolt vanishes, then it's replaced with an orange glow. Like the familiars. Fire, enemy of space existence, seems to be a hallmark for Sax on this station. He wants to laugh at this, but the act is exhausting, so he lays there instead.

Watches.

The catwalk, loosened as its connection with the outer ring falls away, begins to crumble. The burning ball that had been Dalachite rolls off the slant, falling towards Sax. Slowly, of course, as the gravity here is a bare fraction of what it is even elsewhere on the station, where *Cobalt*'s spin keeps down and up in existence. Falling after it is a shape he knows; the human. The flames curl around her, skin unburnt, and Sax is confused for a moment before he remembers her mask.

She'll survive. The specimen.

Bas will be proud of him.

43 / CHOICES MADE

Burning searing bright and black. That's what I fall into. That's what should kill me in my slow, twisting descent. I reach with my arms, my legs, trying to find some purchase as the world ignites around me. I close my eyes and expect pain, but feel none of it. A slight warmth, like Ignos on my skin. No puckering blisters, the fire's torching pain.

The mask.

As I roll off Dalachite's carcass, popping and bubbling as everything inside the creature bursts and boils, the mask keeps me insulated. Instead, I see the blue and red and white and orange flickers as they roast the monster around me. The catwalk we're resting on groans, then snaps and collapses and I fall further still. Down towards the vents and terminals that make up the spherical walls of the room.

Dalachite's limbs, those long stretchy things going from its body to the outer sides, shrivel up, disintegrate into ashen clouds. I realize somewhere in this that I'm screaming, but the crackle and pops of snapping metal, the hissing whispers of cooking skin drown out my voice.

I manage to twist so that I'm looking where I'm falling, and catch myself on the sloped side of the sphere. The terminals are smooth to the touch, with the only purchase coming in the small gaps between the screens.

I slide, slow, towards the bottom. Blackened bits of metal and things I don't recognize tumble around me. Cling to the mask, to me.

Then it's done. Everything settles. Burning bits of viscera and debris litter the bottom of the sphere. I pick out one thing in the middle of that. A large body. The Oratus, Sax. He's lying there, his right claws holding Coorvin's weapon, dead silent.

I see the broad burn in his torso, and other wounds scarring his skin. The creature has had a tough time of it. I don't know what it takes to kill one of these things, but it certainly looks like Sax has met that mark.

"Are you alive?" the voice comes from above. Coorvin, the strange fur-covered thing, the one who'd been holding his head, seemingly incapable of speaking, stares at me from the ledge by the door.

Where the catwalk had once connected, a memory marked by a jagged set of torn beams and bars.

"I don't know," I say.

Because the truth is I don't know what's happening. I can feel myself breathe, I can feel the side of the sphere through the mask, and I think, maybe, I'm not in danger.

You are. Without Dalachite, Cobalt will slowly die. You need to get off the station.

Ignos jerks me back. It's still in my mind, and it's speaking clear, but leaving the station means getting out of here, back to the shuttle.

"Do you have a way to get me up?" I ask Coorvin.

The little creature looks around, then back at me. Shakes its head.

"Can you jump?" Coorvin asks.

I haven't considered making a leap for the ledge. Everything seems to float here, so I might be able to make it. To attempt that, I'll need to get to the other side of the sphere. Back over towards Coorvin. So I walk, one foot after another, stepping over the broken, twisted bits.

Stepping over Sax.

I notice something, staring down at those gray scales, at the vents that line his chest. He's shuddering. His claws twitching slightly. Is the Oratus alive?

It doesn't matter. Leave him.

Ignos had sent me on the quest to find and kill the two Oratus. Claimed they were a mortal threat to me and my friends. Yet Sax saved my life. He destroyed Dalachite before it devoured me, had tried to help Malo and Viera.

Before I really think about it, I bend over, grab the Oratus' claws with my hands and pull. Sax is like a large log. If we were home, I'm sure I couldn't move him, but here he slides ever so slightly along the smooth metal, dragging ash with him as he goes.

"Coorvin, I need help," I shout. "He's still alive."

This agitates the furry creature, who watches as I pull Sax close to the upward sloping side. The part of the sphere beneath the ledge. I'm almost there when noises begin to ring out; sharp clanging sounds unnatural and strange, and when I look around, I can't find the cause.

"Alarms!" Coorvin shouts. "Without Dalachite, Cobalt's systems can't work. We have to leave now!"

"Not without the Oratus!" I reply, and ask Ignos what 'systems' Coorvin is talking about.

There are countless ones that may need constant maintenance. That sound might mean something simple, like a familiar asking for an order. Or something worse, like an oxygen drain that needs repair before vacuum sucks us all away. Or a course correction before a speeding piece of space debris cuts the station in half.

That doesn't sound good. I look at Sax, limp. If Coorvin can't find something soon, I'll have to leave the Oratus. He helped me, but Sax is also the reason I'm here in the first place.

I see a way, if you're determined to save him.

A way?

The Oratus drug themselves before fights. It's disgusting, but it works. Looks like this one still has his, attached to the mask there. It's a small box, singed on the outside. Down by Sax's waist.

I lean over, pry open the top with my fingers. Inside is what looks like a clear container with a black, smooth seal, one I need a way to pierce. The answer strikes me in the form of a jagged piece of metal. I grab it, stick the piece down through the seal until it's coated with the strange substance. I pull it out. It looks smeared, like tree sap.

I think they eat it.

I hold it near Sax's mouth, but it's closed tight.

I've seen, growing up, wild animals and people playing with them. The creatures would bite without warning, snap and slash, even if they were asleep seconds before. I know what lies behind Sax's lips: all those rows of terrifying teeth, and even if Sax doesn't mean to, he could bite my hand clean off.

But if I don't find some way to wake him up, he'll die.

I begin to push, to pry. Sax's lips are squishy, but, with a bit of force, his jaw moves. Like pushing aside a thick branch. I see the rows and rows of teeth, and in the back, a long twisting tongue curled up on itself.

I stick the metal in, rub it on the tongue. I try to be careful, but the metal is small, I'm nervous, it slips in my fingers, and I see a line of red where it cuts. Sax's eyes fly open, and I jerk back. Fall over and hit the side of the sphere. Catch myself, and watch as the Oratus spasms.

Sax is blinking rapidly, his throat making short hissing noises, and then Sax spits the metal out.

We both lie there, breathing for a moment, then the Oratus looks at me.

"I cannot move my legs," the Oratus hisses, and bits of blood drip from between his lips as he does. "You have to pull me."

"I don't have the strength," I say.

"Use the Stim," Sax replies.

There's a banging from above. It's Coorvin, and he's dragging a box of supplies. He drops it, and it floats down to me. Comes to a rest on the floor of the sphere. Before I can ask what he's doing, Coorvin runs off again. I turn back to the Oratus. His claw is resting on his

Stim pack, and I watch it break the seal, digging deep, glistening when it comes back out.

"Come closer," Sax says.

I don't want to. I don't know what that drug is going to do to me, but what are my alternatives? Dying here?

So I crawl on my hands and knees to keep from sliding on the metal. Sax sticks the claw towards me, holds it steady, and I lick it. The same way I would a stick of sugar cane. The same way I might get the last bit of juice from a split melon. The stuff tastes sweet, it pops in my mouth.

And then I'm a new human.

44 / RESURGENCE

Sax watches the human take the Stim. He's not sure how the creature's body will handle it. It's a small dose, barely enough to see an Oratus through a quick fight. Yet these species, if the Amigga's tests are right, only have one heart. Their bodies are smaller, fragile. The last thing Sax wants right now is for Kaishi to explode. For her muscles to twitch too hard and fast and snap or spin out of control. He's seen that before with Flaum, ones who thought they could find an advantage by overindulging in Stim's power.

Other Flaum had to clean up the mess that experiment left behind.

Kaishi's eyes blink rapidly for a few seconds, then close as she shudders, but she appears to stay alive. There's another crunch as a second crate falls, piling against the first. Sax understands what Coorvin is doing: creating a ladder, steps of the sort that the Oratus and human can use to climb out of the sphere. Kaishi, with the Stim, will still need to push Sax up.

"Now pull," Sax says. "Drag me to the boxes, and then lift me up."

Kaishi nods at him, and then reaches out, grips his forearm, and starts to drag Sax. The Oratus helps when he can, using his tail and his midclaws to push himself along. Together they get over to the two crates Coorvin has dropped as the Flaum pushes a third one off.

They're resting on each other, with the base pushing against the bulk of the collapsed catwalk at the bottom of the sphere.

Kaishi uses the crates, gripping the one and then another, and pulling herself, and then Sax after her, until they're on the top of the stack. Now they're only two meters beneath the ledge where Coorvin stands, watching them.

Sax plunges his claws into the flat faces of the terminals on the side in front of them. Shatters their screens, punctures the gray metal slates, and tries to climb, but even with the Stim, his arms quiver; he can barely hold himself up, which means lifting is out of the question.

Beneath him, Kaishi pushes. Thrusts Sax up until the Oratus manages, with one outstretched lunge of his foreclaws, to grip the edge of the ledge. Coorvin scrambles over, grab's Sax's right foreclaw with his hands and tugs. The power is so pathetic that Sax wants to laugh, but every little bit helps.

"Climb me," Sax hisses down to Kaishi, who, after hesitating for a moment, obliges.

She jumps onto Sax's tail and clamors up the Oratus' body. Sax takes a foot to the face without whining. Without biting it off.

Restraint Bas would admire.

Kaishi gets up on the ledge, turns and looks at him, holds out a hand.

"If I reach for it, I'll fall," Sax hisses.

"You have a better idea?" Kaishi replies.

"My tail," Sax says. "Get ready to grab it."

Kaishi lies down, chest on the ledge. Coorvin moves near her, hands at the ready. Sax swings his tail from left to right, back and forth, going farther and farther, building momentum, and then, moving right, Sax lets his left foreclaw loose, allowing his body to swing with the tail. Kaishi and Coorvin pull as Sax swings around, scraping Sax's chest against and over the edge of the ledge. Sax clamps down his right foreclaw and midclaw as Kaishi and Coorvin dash and hold his tail and pull the Oratus the rest of the way onto the platform.

He's up.

Which leaves room for the next crisis.

The alarms are deafening now, and coming in a thousand tones and beats. What terminals remain are flashing reds and yellows. *Cobalt* itself seems to be shivering. They can't stay here. Sax pushes himself onto his tail. He still can't feel his legs, and he looks down to confirm they exist. Kaishi and Coorvin place themselves beneath his midclaws, supporting the Oratus on their shoulders. Together the three of them walk from the sphere and leave Dalachite to its final resting place.

They trudge along the hallway, through the room where the familiars were made, and two of the chambers beyond. Until they come to a sealed door, next to a now-ruined screen Sax remembers showing the progress of the Amigga's experiments.

Sax has enough strength for this, with the Stim still pulsing through his blood. He takes his four claws, drives them into the sides of the door.

"Pull me!" Sax hisses.

Kaishi and Coorvin shove the Oratus hard, and Sax adds what he can of his own muscle. The claws rend the metal away, and the door falls towards him to show, on the other side, two humans. One, Malo, is still wrapped in bars on the table. The other, Viera, holds the remnants of another bar like some sort of weapon, eyes wild and ready to swing.

"Kaishi, you're alive!" Viera yells.

But the human's face turns as she sees Sax collapse, eyes closed, to the floor.

45 / *LEAVING IT BEHIND*

I pick Sax up again, Viera helping Coorvin and I. We drag him to Malo's body, and though Sax seems barely alive, we use his claws like knives to cut the metal keeping Malo tied down. The Charre warrior springs up and replaces me under Sax, sharing the burden with Viera.

"What happened?" Viera's asking, and I say I'll fill them in as we go.

The walk through the station is slow. Every so often we come across familiars; leftovers, plain blue, standing silent and eerie. Not reacting, not moving or noticing us. We pass by the kitchen, and there's no food ready to serve. No sign of violence. We don't go back to our quarters—nothing there worth grabbing. Only to the docking bay. To the shuttle, to our escape.

Evidence of the failing station manifests in flickering lights, in locked doors sealing passages and glowing red. The sounds echo back and forth down the hallways, chiming off of each other in a haunting dissonance that makes me wish for the natural jungle cries of my home. I knew what those meant. These noises are alien, and frightening.

Sax, limp and staving off death, hisses strange things. Stuff about power supplies and unstable reactions.

"Do you know what he's talking about?" I ask Coorvin.

"Like all stations, *Cobalt* demands modulated power. Most of the time it can function on its own, but Dalachite has been making so many changes, the station might not be able to survive without its guidance. *Cobalt* might be breaking apart."

"Kaishi, we should leave him and go," Viera says, her breath is faint. I'd forgotten that she almost died not that long ago.

"He saved me, Viera," I reply. "Hurt himself trying to save us. We're not leaving him."

"Honor demands we help," Malo adds.

That keeps Viera quiet, keeps us all moving until we get to the docking bay. Until we get to the ruin. Slumped against the shuttle is Bas, two miners in her mid-claws, resting amid a horde of burned and broken familiars. Charred lumps of blue goop mark the end of a tough fight. Bas has her share of wounds; She's bleeding from cuts, and plenty of her pink-gold scales have been knocked off, damaged. Yet as we enter, she raises one miner towards us.

"Does he live?" Her hisses are weak, tired.

I step forward. "He's alive. He saved me, and we killed the Amigga."

Bas gives me a slow nod. "I could tell when they stopped coming."

"What happened here?" Malo asks.

"Had to keep the shuttle safe. It's our only way off the station."

Take it. I can tell you how to fly. Leave the Oratus. They'll kill you as soon as they recover.

I blink.

They took you before. What do you think will happen now? They won't let you go. They'll take you somewhere else. Somewhere worse than here.

I feel sick all of a sudden. Torn. My eyes find Viera and Malo's, and they're waiting for my decision. Waiting for me to help them bring Bas and Sax into the shuttle.

But I think Ignos is right. Either one of them, Sax or Bas, could kill us all by themselves. Or take us to another station like this one. I remember the sessions, remember the pain the terror.

I can take you home, Kaishi. All of you.

"Coorvin." I look at the Flaum. "Are there other ways off of the station?"

"There are several evacuation modules," Coorvin replies. "But I don't know why you'd want to use them with this shuttle right here."

You see? No need to take the risk.

"Come on, let's move," I say. Viera and Malo go to lift Sax, but I shake my head. I hear a sharp hiss, and see Bas has her miner trained on me. "I'm sorry. You can try to kill us now if you want but we're leaving in that shuttle."

"Kaishi?" Malo asks. "What are you saying?"

"Ignos is right. There's a risk, Malo. The Oratus brought us here, they won't let us go. If we want to head home, then we can't bring them with us. Coorvin says there are other ways off the station. We don't need to take them."

"I can't let you leave," Bas says. "Not with that thing in your mind."

She raises the miner, pulls the trigger, but nothing happens. It's empty. Bas doesn't even look surprised, just defeated.

"I'm sorry," I say, and then Viera, Malo and I head towards the shuttle. Up the boarding ramp inside, which, with Ignos telling me how, I shut, leaving our kidnappers behind.

46 / TO SPACE

Sax can't protest as the humans walk pass him onto the shuttle. He watches, his nerves flickering, trying to establish contact with his legs. The shuttle ramp slides up, and not long after a hum fills the air as the shuttle's engines turn on.

"You let them go," Sax says in a burst of breath to Bas.

"The miner was out of charge," Bas replies.

"You had another."

"To do what?" Bas, still resting against the shuttle strut, says. "Hurt them? Kill them?"

"Keep them here?"

"They wouldn't have gone with us willingly. They would've died, and then this would all be useless. We know where they're going. We can follow them."

Bas makes a good point. If they're going back to the human's planet, they'll be easy enough to find. To track down again. But that means the Oratus have to live long enough to do so.

The shuttle shakes and the struts begin to move. Bas falls to the ground as her support pulls away. She drops her miners and drags herself towards Sax. Who, himself, with the help of Coorvin pulling him along, heads towards the door out of the bay. They have to leave before the magnetic shield lowers for the shuttle. Before vacuum sucks them into space.

Whomever flies the ship isn't an experienced pilot: the shuttle goes up slowly, gets a meter or so off of the ground before doing a lazy turn around. Plenty of time for Coorvin, Sax and Bas to make it to the door and back through. To slam it shut and seal them in the hallway.

There's a familiar standing there, staring at them, unmoving.

"The evac modules are this way," Coorvin says.

The Flaum doesn't seem perturbed in the least that Kaishi took the shuttle. Then again, he's spent so long on the station, Coorvin might just be happy to leave, no matter how.

There's a low rumble, a churning beneath the continual blaring of alarms, as the shuttle rockets out through the bay.

"We're in deep space," Sax says. "There's no habitable planets around?"

"You know what it was like with Dalachite?" Coorvin says, his voice high and jittering, yet somehow solemn. "That thing dominated the station. Drove away the staff and replaced it with familiars. It experimented on all of us, and it nearly took my mind. Now I'm free to go find someplace new. To get off the station. The evac mods give us a chance, so I'm going to take it. You're welcome to come with."

"Then let's go," Sax hisses.

They head through to the station towards the evac mods. The smell of ozone and burning electronics fills the air. *Cobalt* is falling apart without Dalachite, its heart and soul.

"What did the Amigga want?" Bas asks Coorvin as they go.

"Dalachite wasn't the only one looking for these things," Coorvin shudders as he speaks, as he walks. "They communicated. All of the Amigga. The familiars are a test, a way to remove the need for us."

"Us?"

"Species are unpredictable, Dalachite told me. They need, they want. Familiars have neither of those things. They will obey without question, and on a large scale."

"Then why not machines?"

"I don't know," Coorvin replies. "I didn't really have conversations with Dalachite. More like it ranted at me."

They reach the trio of circular doors, each one leading to its own evac mod. Coorvin takes them to the one on the left, punches the panel, and the door slides open. Inside are a pair of benches and a lot of bound packages full of rations and water. Medical supplies. Enough to last for quite some time. They head inside, Sax and Bas working to arrange themselves in the least painful way possible, breaking into the packs of healing salves, bandages and beginning to patch themselves back to life.

"Ready?" Coorvin says.

"Launch us," Sax hisses.

With a few quick presses, the mod is shut tight, and a second later they blast off into space.

47 / ONE LAST LEAP

I stare into the black infinite and realize I have no idea what I'm doing.

Beneath my hands are a string of terminals not too unlike what I saw in the Amigga's chamber. Screens displaying graphs and what look like maps. One scrolls a message full of names I don't know or understand. From someone named Evva. Ignos tells me to ignore it. To ignore everything except for a single screen on the far right side. I have to step over there to reach it, as it's clear the shuttle is meant for longer arms, larger bodies. Malo and Viera, behind me, stare around dumbfounded.

I can't imagine what this would be like without a voice in my head explaining everything.

This is the part we need to use. It sets the leap trajectory. A folding of the universe around the ship to move us where we need to go.

Then again, maybe having a voice in your head doesn't help all that much.

I'm going to give you a series of numbers, and you need to enter them precisely as I tell you.

Part of the display holds a series of circles with numbers inside, going zero through nine. To the left of the number pad is what looks like a glowing sphere of bright points. Things that, if you shot them in the night sky, would resemble the stars Ignos says they are. Ignos reads off the numbers, and I don't know where he's getting them from, but I enter them anyway. Press my finger on the little circles representing each digit. As I complete the entry, the stars in the display begin to shift. To zoom in and narrow until one isolated region is represented. It's clearly a map, though of what I'm not sure.

The galaxy, Kaishi. What lies beyond the sky of home.

A home we're going back to. I turn to Malo and Viera. "I've entered the directions Ignos gave me," I say. "We're going home."

You should strap in.

I look around. There's no clear way to do that. No seats, or anything to hold. The bridge holds only tiled metal floor and terminals.

You have to hit the button first.

I glance back at the display, and the number pad has transformed into two square blocks of color. One green, the other red.

The green one.

I touch it, and there's a pleasant sounding chime. The broad window grays out, and then a giant number 10 appears. It begins to count down. The floor beneath my feet and the ceiling above my hands rotates, and shiny black webbing dangles from above, while thick bars slide over and across pairs of tiles on the floor.

You must step between them.

"Put your feet underneath the straps," I say, stepping into my own.

When I slide my foot between two of the strapped tiles, a bright green light flashes, and then the strap restricts until it almost hurts, pinning my foot to the floor. The same thing happens with my other foot when I shift it in.

Above me, the netting slides down. It fits to me; molding around my back. I feel something click behind my feet. It's almost like I'm standing in a hammock, a comfort I sometimes had back home—thick mossweaves hung between two trees.

The counter reaches zero.

"This is what we did before, isn't it?" I ask Ignos.

It doesn't have time to answer. The universe warps and splits. My stomach slides into and out of itself, my head bursts with ringing confusion. The gray in front of me turns a broad white, then a rainbow of color splashes across, as if I'm spinning quickly through a room of flowers. It fades just as fast, turns back to black. To a star-filled expanse, one giant, entirely tan circle in front of us, wisps of gray scattered over its surface.

I'm breathing hard, but coming back from this leap is not the disaster of the first. I'm ready in a few seconds. Even Viera and Malo aren't crying. Aren't panicking, though I notice Viera's fists are clenched tight against the netting.

Is this it? Are we home?

Of course.

Kaishi's adventures continue in Clarity's Dawn —read on for an excerpt, or find more adventures at Black Key Books:

AN EXCERPT FROM CLARITY'S DAWN

THE SKYWARD SAGA BOOK THREE

The ship shudders as it begins its docking phase. The magnetic gravity decreases to prevent interference with *Scrapper Station*'s own systems, and Bas, with a flick of her tail, sends a pile of gray-metal tiles floating through the air.

"We'll find a way to contact Evva from the station," Bas says, her eyes tracking the chips. "She'll know how to get us back home."

The two of them share the space for a while longer, feeling every part of the docking process in the freighter's shakes. It takes far longer to dock a ship of this size than it does the shuttle Sax and Bas used to fly—the freighter's too large to simply fit in a bay. Instead, *Scrapper Station* uses a series of arms to 'catch' the ship, once the freighter matches the station's velocity, and then it extends a long tube to the passenger airlock.

When that tube connects, the door to the Oratus' room shunts open, and for the first time Sax is face-to-face with Plake. The Vyphen is half Sax's height, and her red skin shimmers beneath the thick white and yellow feathers running along her back and arms. In low gravity, and on the small world the Vyphens called home, Plake could fly.

Not that it would help her escape Sax's claws in tight quarters like these. By her eyes, narrowed and deep green, Plake knows this. But she doesn't crouch away, flinch, or clench her webbed hands when Sax glares down at her.

Plake has the respect of her crew, and Sax begins to see why.

Agra-Red and one of the black-furred Flaum stand behind Plake, both with miners trained on the Oratus. Backing up their commander's courage with the firepower it deserves.

"You'll follow me," Plake says. "They'll follow you. Let's go."

As they leave the room, Sax hears the churning, banging, shifting noise of unloading cargo. He throws a look over the railing and back down the deep bay. Bright white lights pierce the soft yellow of the freighter's illumination, showing where the robo-skiffs are working. Grabbing crates with their magnet arms, floating with them to the bay's cargo airlock, where, after pressure's drained, the skiffs would take their goodies across a short expanse to the station.

"I thought those were meant for *Cobalt*," Sax says to Plake's back as they move.

"*Cobalt* doesn't exist anymore," Plake replies without turning her head. "Figure that makes them mine to sell."

"Does the Chorus agree?"

"Who's going to tell them? You?"

Sax bares his teeth, though the Vyphen can't see it. He doesn't need Bas' tail tap to keep his mouth shut this time.

The connection tube doesn't give them much more than a view, through thick glass, of the station. It's enough to tell Sax why *Scrapper Station* has its name—built in the aftermath of a thick Vincere-Sevora battle, *Scrapper Station* looks like someone swept up a bunch of junk and glued it all together. There's no semblance of organization, no planning—the station shoots out in all directions, with jutting points and nodes veering out into space.

There's no planet near here, which means no gravity grabbing all these lanky parts. Only asteroids, stocked with valuable metals and the reason for the fight in the first place. As they walk, Sax can see small mining ships blasting to and from tiny bays, grabbing platinum and gold from spinning rocks and returning it. A big refiner craft, like Plake's freighter, is doing its own docking procedure. It's shaped like a cylinder, and the raw ore will be loaded into one end, refined during the trip, and the cleaned product will be ready on delivery to whatever crafters want it.

"There's more here than I expected," Bas says.

"None of you know what's going on in the galaxy you're trying to protect," Plake replies. "You see all those little guys? Grabbing the metals? They're supplying you with all your weapons. One run at a time."

"Would you rather we focused on this station than the Sevora?" Sax cuts in. "We're keeping you alive."

"By destroying *Cobalt*? Didn't think it was the enemy."

Sax doesn't have an answer for that. It would be easy to say Dalachite tried to kill them, that it was performing strange, reprehensible experiments, but the galaxy depends on its hierarchy and the Amigga stand at the top. Undermining their authority goes against everything Sax, and those who fight in the Vincere, stand for.

So he marches in silence until they're through the tube, passing through a dented door—evidence, perhaps, of a few desperate entry attempts—and into one of *Scrapper Station*'s arrival areas.

Rather than the cluster of species mingling their way back and forth, dealing in promises both physical and not, the wide room stands deserted except for a trio. Two of them, crag-like Lutos, hold large miners in their black-dirt arms. The single-eyed, mud-coated monsters don't talk much, and Sax is surprised to see any of them outside of their molten puddle of a home planet.

"Just as you promised, Plake," the voice comes from the third, the only species capable of talking, a yellow mound with a pair of stalked, bulbous eyes. "I'll take them."

The Ooblot says the words. Sax is ready to dodge, but the fire doesn't come from in front, from the Lutos. No, the searing pain, the numbing shock that sends the Oratus down into black strikes from behind.

Continue the adventure with Clarity's Dawn available now:

ACKNOWLEDGMENTS

This novel is the product of my family and friends refusing to let a dream die. My wife Nicole, for letting me write in the early mornings and making sure I didn't starve. My brothers and parents for their continual comments, support, and enthusiasm.

And, of course, you, the reader, for giving me a reason to write.

ABOUT THE AUTHOR

A.R. Knight spins stories in a frosty house in Madison, WI, primarily owned by a pair of cats. After getting sucked into the working grind in the economic crash of the 2008, he found himself spending boring meetings soaring through space and going on grand adventures.

Eventually, spending time with podcasting, screenplays, short stories and other novels, he found a story he could fall into and a cast of characters both entertaining and full of heart.

Thanks, as always, for reading!

For more information:
www.adamrknight.com

To Anna and Elsa, the cats whose fluffy fur blankets keep the winter writing warm

ISBNs:
Ebook: 978-1-946554-24-6
Paperback: 978-1-946554-42-0
Hardcover: 979-8-88858-058-5
Large Print: 979-8-88858-059-2
Published by Black Key Books

This is a work of fiction. Any similarity between the characters and situations within its pages and places or persons, living or dead, is unintentional and co-incidental.

www.blackkeybooks.com

www.ingramcontent.com/pod-product-compliance
Lightning Source LLC
Chambersburg PA
CBHW030618310726
48979CB00003B/773

* 9 7 9 8 8 8 8 5 8 0 5 8 5 *